More praise for
STONE RIVER CROSSING

"Tim Tingle's sure-footed storytelling in Stone River Crossing offers up action, humor, suspense, and a tolerable amount of romance. This historical novel is a deft blending of the supernatural and the everyday as well as a timely reminder that we're all in this together."

—**Chris Barton**, author of
Shark vs. Train and *Whoosh!*

"Only master Choctaw storyteller Tim Tingle could create such a moving tale of friendship reaching across the Bok Chitto River."

—**Dawn Quigley**, PhD,
Turtle Mountain Ojibwe Nation,
author of *Apple in the Middle*

STONE RIVER CROSSING

TIM TINGLE

Tu Books
An Imprint of LEE & LOW BOOKS Inc.
New York

Copyright © 2019 by Tim Tingle

TU BOOKS, an imprint of LEE & LOW BOOKS Inc.,
95 Madison Avenue, New York, NY 10016

leeandlow.com

Manufactured in the United States of America by Worzalla Publishing Company

Book design by Neil Swaab

Cover art by Julie Flett

Typesetting by ElfElm Publishing

Book production by The Kids at Our House

The text is set in Bembo MT Pro and Nobbin

10 9 8 7 6 5 4 3 2 1

First Edition

Cataloging-in-Publication Data is on file with the Library of Congress

are," she said aloud. "No one will see me once I'm on the other side."

Martha Tom had been warned. They all had. The words of her mother seemed to ripple the calm waters.

On the other side of the river lies danger, nothing but danger. You are not to cross the river, ever. The nahullos, the white people, keep slaves to do their work. If you don't want to be their slave, stay away from the river.

Lured by the blackberries, Martha Tom shook her head and made the warnings go away. She tucked the cane basket under her arm and took a deep breath. With one final look to make certain she was alone, she lifted her skirt and stepped into the river—to the crossing path beneath the waters.

One careful step at a time, Martha Tom crept across the river. The path she trod was a path of stones, impossible to see and rising from the dark river bottom.

The stones rose *almost* to the top of the river. So that no one could see them—no one but Choctaws—they had built the walkway a foot below the surface of the muddy river, hidden from view. Only the Choctaws knew of the stones.

Once, when she was five years old, Martha Tom was caught playing on the stone walkway, slipping and falling and swimming to the shore.

"Never do that again!" her mother had warned her.

I can't think about that or I'll drown, Martha Tom thought. *I'm older now. I'm alone, and no one will ever know about today.*

She stepped from the stones to the other shore and soon found a blackberry vine, drooping with fat purple berries. She plucked the first berry and tossed it into her mouth, smacking at the tart, delicious taste.

"Mmmm, juicy and almost sweet," she said. Hunger gnawed at her belly. She ate another.

The first taste of breakfast made her crave more, and Martha Tom ate another berry. *Mmmm.*

She picked five more berries, placed them in her basket—then one by one popped them in her mouth! When she'd eaten every blackberry in the bushes, she licked her fingers and wiped the juice from her lips. She spotted another clump of blackberries, only a short distance into the woods.

She soon ate them all.

Deeper into the woods she walked, stooping and picking and tasting her way from one berry vine to another. She lost all track of time. When both the basket and her stomach were full, she looked to the sky. She'd hoped to see smoke rising from the Choctaw cooking fires, but the sky was cloudy, and the trees blocked her view.

With a shiver of fear, Martha Tom realized she was lost. She remembered her mother's warnings. *Martha Tom, you cannot play by the river. You must not be seen on the*

4

path. The plantation guards will capture you. They will make you a slave, just like the field workers.

Martha Tom wrapped her arms around the basket and ran.

I can't be far from the river, she thought.

She burst through the woods into a huge man-made clearing, with trees uprooted and branches sawed off. *I'm nowhere near the river! I might never make it home.*

CHAPTER 2

Martha Tom Meets Lil Mo

Martha Tom was more afraid than ever. Fat tears rolled down her cheeks. She lifted her face and studied the clearing.

Row after row of logs, almost like benches, stretched from one end of the clearing to the other. A sawed-off tree stump stood only a few feet in front of her, surrounded by grapevines. Martha Tom wiped away the tears and sat on the stump.

"I'll wait here till after dark," she said. "The clouds will be gone by then and I can find my way home by the moon."

The sound of cracking branches broke her thoughts. Someone was coming.

Martha Tom dove headfirst into the grapevines.

A skinny, dark-skinned man appeared, hobbling on a

cane. He stooped when he walked, and rings of white hair fell from beneath his black hat.

Martha Tom watched as he leaned his cane against the stump and slowly, painfully, climbed to the top. He steadied himself, then looked right and left. He lifted his arms as if waving at people, but they were alone.

Or so it seemed.

What happened next would change Martha Tom's life forever. The man turned his palms upward and pointed to the trees to his right.

"I am bound for the promised land!" he shouted.

Martha Tom followed his gaze. She saw no one. The leaves bristled, and the tree limbs swayed. Then she heard the voices.

I am bound for the promised land . . .

"Spirit people!" Martha Tom whispered, clapping her hand over her mouth and hoping he had not heard.

He had not. He glanced to his left. "I am bound for the promised land!" he shouted again.

Once more, even louder, the voices sang.

I am bound for the promised land . . .

"Oh, who will come and go with me?" the old man

called, raising both arms high and bowing his head.

"*We will come and go with you*," replied the voices, lifting like clouds from every tree and bush.

Martha Tom wrapped her arms around her knees, closed her eyes tight, and whispered a prayer. "Please make this morning go away. Let me wake up and be home. I will never disobey my mother again, I promise."

When Martha Tom opened her eyes, the morning was more alive than ever. People of every age stepped from the trees and entered the clearing. They were families of the enslaved field workers, mothers and fathers and children, and they sang as they walked.

> *I am bound for the promised land,*
> *I am bound for the promised land,*
> *O, who will come and go with me?*
> *I am bound for the promised land.*

Martha Tom had never heard music like this before. Everyone sang in beautiful harmony, swaying with the music. It was the calling together of the forbidden slave church, deep in the Mississippi woods. The old man on the stump nodded and everyone stood still, heads bowed and hands clasped together.

Martha Tom froze, hoping no one saw her.

A soft finger tapped her on the shoulder, and she jerked

in fear. The biggest man she had ever seen stood over her.

"Are you lost?" he asked.

"Yes," she whispered.

"You're Choctaw, from across the river Bok Chitto?"

Martha Tom nodded.

"You are scared, aren't you?"

Martha Tom *was* scared, and when she tried to speak, the words refused to come.

"You want to go home?"

She nodded, ten times in a moment, and the man smiled.

"What is your name?"

"Martha Tom."

"Well, Martha Tom," he said, kneeling beside her, "you don't have to be afraid. No one will hurt you. I'll call my son, and he can take you to the river." He stood up, looked to the crowd of worshippers, and shouted, "Lil Mo! Come here, son."

A thin boy of about ten appeared. He looked back and forth from his father to this strange little girl.

"Lil Mo," his father said, "this is Martha Tom. She's Choctaw, from across the river. She is lost and afraid. Take her to the riverbank and come back right away. She can find her way across."

"I better not," Lil Mo said, shaking his head. "I'm afraid for us, Papa. The guards always tell us to stay away from the

river. They say our whole family will get in trouble if they find us there. They'd think we were trying to escape."

"Son, son," his father said, touching Lil Mo on the shoulder. "There is a way to move amongst them where they won't even see you. I should have already taught you, but it's time you learned. You walk *not too fast, not too slow, keep your eyes to the ground, away you go*. No one will even see you. It'll be like you're invisible. Now, get this little girl to the river."

Lil Mo stared at the ground, letting his father know he didn't want to go to the river. "Papa," he whispered, lifting his face to look at him.

His father gave him a look that said *do not disobey me*.

Lil Mo nodded and took Martha Tom by the hand. She stood up slowly, biting her lip. She was embarrassed to stand before the churchgoers, but they waved and smiled at her. Martha Tom gave a small wave in reply.

"Come on," said Lil Mo. "And remember what my papa said. *Not too fast, not too slow, eyes to the ground, away we go!*"

———

Lil Mo knew the way to the river, and they soon stood on the shore. "Here we are," he said. "Where's your boat?"

"I don't have a boat," said Martha Tom.

"Then how did you cross the river?"

"A secret way," said Martha Tom. "Can you keep a secret?"

"Little girl, I am the best secret keeper you will ever meet," said Lil Mo. This Choctaw girl *was* strange, but Lil Mo was beginning to like her.

"I hope you can keep a secret," said Martha Tom, "because I'm not supposed to show anybody what I'm about to show you. Follow me." She walked down to the riverbank till she came to a muddy spot covered with footprints.

"Are those footprints yours?" asked Lil Mo.

"Yes."

"So how did you cross the river?" he asked.

"You're about to see," she said. "Here, hold the basket."

Lil Mo took the basket and watched as Martha Tom took ten steps from the river, then turned to face him. "What are you doing?" he asked.

Without answering him, Martha Tom took a deep breath, nodded at Lil Mo, and took off running to the river.

"Little girl, you better slow down!" Lil Mo shouted. "I'm not gonna jump in the water and save you. I can't swim and carry you at the same time!"

Martha Tom leapt from the shore and landed on the water. She wavered back and forth, but only for a

moment. Once her footing was firm, she turned slowly to Lil Mo and smiled.

His jaw dropped, and his eyes were as big as chicken eggs.

"You are a witch," he said in a trembling voice. "Please don't hurt me. I promise not to tell anybody, just leave me alone."

CHAPTER 3

Walking on the Water

Martha Tom laughed, and Lil Mo slowly backed away.

"Don't go, Lil Mo," she said. "I'm not a witch. Here, let me show you."

"No," said Lil Mo. "I'm going home."

"Wait! Please. I would never hurt you, Lil Mo. Your father saved my life."

Lil Mo hesitated, staring at the strange little girl standing on the water.

"I know this river," he said. "I come here sometimes at night. Me and a friend sneak away. Where you're standing is deep water, so how can you tell me you're not a witch?"

"I'm standing on a stone path," she said. "The stones cross from one side of the river to the other. Lil Mo, I want to show you the crossing place. But you cannot tell anyone. Promise?"

"I promise."

"Good. Now, just step right here," Martha Tom said, pointing to the water beneath her feet. "Don't be afraid."

"Nooo." Lil Mo shook his head.

"Lil Mo, you have to trust me."

Lil Mo looked into her face. He had never trusted anyone of a different color. "Why should I?"

"Because your father saved my life, that's why. If the people from the plantation house found me first, they wouldn't let me go home."

"Why not?" Lil Mo asked.

"You don't know, do you?" said Martha Tom. The river flowed beneath her as she talked. "Lil Mo, who do you think were their slaves before they brought your people here?"

Lil Mo tilted his head. "Who?"

"We were their slaves," said Martha Tom. "My people, the Choctaw people, we were their slaves. But they couldn't keep us. We know these woods better than anyone. We could run away and hide. That's what my grandfather says."

Lil Mo looked up at her and smiled. "You and your Choctaw people know these woods better than anyone?"

Martha Tom nodded.

"So, Little Miss Choctaw I-Know-These-Woods-

Better-Than-Anyone, why did I have to bring you to the river?" he asked with a smile.

Martha Tom laughed for the first time all day. "You are a funny boy," she said. "But do you see now why you can trust me? Your father saved my life." She pointed to the water. "Here, step here. Go slow at first, till you feel the stone."

Lil Mo eased his foot through the muddy water. He couldn't see the path, but he trusted Martha Tom. When his foot felt the stone, a grin crept across his face. "A miracle," he said. "This is a miracle. How could I not know about this path? How could *we* not know?"

Step by step, Martha Tom led Lil Mo across the river Bok Chitto.

"How long has the path been here?" he asked.

"I don't know," said Martha Tom. "Maybe forever."

So the path to freedom is always there, he thought, *if you learn to see it.* Then he smiled, realizing he still couldn't see the path. "Only by my trust," he whispered.

CHAPTER 4

The Strangest Wedding Ever (for Lil Mo)

Even before they stepped from the stones to the shore, Lil Mo heard a song in the distance.

"What is that?" he asked.

"That's the friendship chant," said Martha Tom. "The old men are singing the song and calling everyone to the wedding. Follow me and hurry!"

Martha Tom leapt to the shore and dashed through the trees, clutching her basket tight so she didn't spill any blackberries.

"Wedding? Wait!" shouted Lil Mo.

"No waiting today!" Martha Tom called over her shoulder. "Just keep up. You can run, can't you?"

"Yes, I can run," said Lil Mo. "I can outrun you!"

Lil Mo soon realized that outrunning Martha Tom was not his real problem. He didn't know where he was going and she did—that was the problem. She knew the crawl-spots under fences. She knew the winding paths through thorny bushes.

Soon he found himself standing in a grove of pine trees, alone. "Martha Tom!" he shouted. "I don't like this. I'm going back to the river."

"I'm here," said Martha Tom, stepping out from behind a tree.

"Why did you do that?"

"I was just playing, Lil Mo," said Martha Tom. "I'm home now. I don't have to be afraid anymore."

"That's no reason to make *me* afraid!"

Martha Tom smiled. "Lil Mo, I want you to meet my family. You can come to the wedding!"

"I better be going," Lil Mo said. "My father and mother will worry."

"You can't go now!" said Martha Tom. "We're almost there."

They walked quickly through the pines and soon stepped onto a street lined with log houses.

"This is a town!" said Lil Mo.

"What did you expect?" asked Martha Tom. "Welcome to Choctaw town, Lil Mo."

"Thank you. I guess."

Martha Tom laughed. "Now, we better hurry. The music has stopped, and the chase is about to begin."

"The chase? I thought we were going to a wedding?"

"A Choctaw wedding, Lil Mo. The man chases the woman, and if he catches her, he can marry her."

"That should be easy," said Lil Mo, then wished he hadn't.

"The woman gets a big head start. If the man doesn't catch her, the wedding is off," Martha Tom explained.

"That doesn't make sense," said Lil Mo.

"It doesn't have to make sense," Martha Tom said, laughing. "It's a wedding!"

Women in beautiful dresses stepped from the log homes, carrying baskets loaded with food. Small children clung to their skirts. Lil Mo and Martha Tom, with hundreds of Choctaws, made their way to a clearing at the end of town. Martha Tom set her basket of berries under a bush and pulled Lil Mo through the crowd.

Lil Mo could not believe what he saw. On the edge of the clearing men played drums and beat small sticks together. In the center of the field stood a small hut, covered with enormous green leaves. Older women surrounded the front door of the hut, and old men circled a door to the rear. A tall pole stood at the end of the clearing.

She hurried through the woods and soon stood on the banks of the Bok Chitto River.

Her eyes scanned up and down the riverbank for blackberries. Thick clumps of vines wrapped around tree trunks and dangled from rocks lining the shore.

Plenty of vines, she thought, *but no berries. They've all been picked.* She strolled up and down the river, brushing aside the prickly vines. *Not a single berry on this side of the river.* She shaded her eyes and gazed to the plantation side.

No one ever picks the berries on that side of the river. They're too busy picking cotton, and the guards never let the slave workers get close to the river.

Martha Tom was forbidden to cross the Bok Chitto River.

She looked over her shoulder at the morning smoke, rising from the cooking fires in Choctaw town. "Everybody's having breakfast. Everybody but me," she whispered to herself. No one was watching.

She tilted her head in curiosity and looked across the river at the plantation shore. *I wonder what life is like for the slaves,* she thought. *They are families like us, with mothers and fathers and children. But the guards have long leather whips and holler at them all day long.*

A ray of morning sunshine sliced through the trees, and a thicket of purple blackberries sparkled in the sun.

"Mother wants me to pick berries, and there they

CHAPTER 1

Stone River Crossing

1808, City of Bok Chitto, Choctaw Nation

"Martha Tom! I have a wedding to cook for today. Get your lazy self out of bed and bring me some blackberries!"

"Oh, Mother," said Martha Tom. She rolled out of bed and put on her dress, stretching and yawning. "No breakfast today?"

"Yes, you can have your breakfast, but not until you fill this basket with blackberries!" her mother said, giving Martha Tom a basket made of river cane. "And hurry back. The wedding is this afternoon."

Martha Tom took the basket and stepped through the back door, wiping her eyes and waking up as she walked.

Mississippi Territory, 1808

Nahullo town

The Mississippi Band
of Choctaw Indians

Choctaw town

Bok Chitto or "Big Water"
(present-day Nanih Way Creek)

Jackson
(present-day capital of
the state of Mississippi)

Pearl River

Present-day Mississippi
state boundaries

To my grandsons,
Finnegan and Niko,
young Choctaws who,
as fluent Spanish speakers,
cross the river daily

"Balili! Balili!" someone shouted.

"Watch, Lil Mo," said Martha Tom. "They're telling her to run."

From the front door came a short woman in a blue-and-white dress. She took a long look at the crowds of people, her Choctaw family and friends. Everyone cheered and shouted, "Balili!"

"She is the bride," Martha Tom said.

"That was my guess," said Lil Mo.

The woman hiked up her skirt and ran, pumping her arms and looking over her shoulder.

"Balili!" called the onlookers.

When the bride was halfway to the pole, the men flung back a deerskin door. Out popped the groom. He wore a blue shirt, the same color as the bride's dress. He was chubby and round, and Lil Mo smiled to think of him trying to catch a woman with a big head start.

"Balili!" shouted the Choctaws, laughing and cheering. The man didn't hesitate. He ducked his head, circled the hut, and ran, churning his legs in a mad dash to catch his bride.

"This wedding is not gonna happen," Lil Mo said.

"Just watch," said Martha Tom.

When she heard the cheers, the bride turned and saw her future husband. Lil Mo expected her to dash to the pole and end the chase, but she didn't. She stopped in her tracks. She clapped her hands and laughed. She jumped up and down. "Balili!" she shouted.

The groom looked up, and a big grin crept across his face.

"Uh-oh," said Lil Mo, pointing to a patch of mud in the groom's path. The groom was eyeing his bride and didn't see what everyone else saw. His feet flew out from under him, and he somersaulted to the ground, rolling over three times before regaining his footing.

"Never gonna happen!" said Lil Mo.

"You have a lot to learn," said Martha Tom.

The bride clapped her hand to her mouth. She took two steps in the direction of her groom, but the women shouted, "No! Balili!"

The bride ran backward, almost falling down herself. When the muddy groom caught his bride—ten feet from the pole—the crowd broke out in happy cheers.

"That was the craziest wedding I ever saw," said Lil Mo.

"That was only the beginning," said Martha Tom. "Follow me."

Soon everyone gathered around the pole. A man with long white hair lifted his arms. The crowd fell silent, and he spoke wedding blessings over the bride and muddy groom.

When the service was complete, Martha Tom's

mother appeared. "Little girl, you have been crossing Bok Chitto!" she said, looking from Martha Tom to Lil Mo. "Who is your friend?"

"Mother, this is Lil Mo," said Martha Tom. She took a deep breath and talked faster than anybody Lil Mo could ever remember, except once when he was in trouble and trying to talk himself out of it.

"I couldn't find any blackberries," said Martha Tom, "and so somehow I found myself lost in the woods on the plantation side of the river, and the next thing I knew, this big man scared me, but he was nice, and he was Lil Mo's father, and Lil Mo is his son, so Lil Mo took me back to the river because I was lost, but now I'm safe. Aren't you glad? Oh, I finally did find enough blackberries to fill the basket, and it's under a bush not far from here, so everything is achukma." Then she turned to Lil Mo. "Achukma means 'good,'" she said with a nod.

"I'm glad you found the berries, and I'm glad you're safe, Martha Tom. I'm glad to meet Lil Mo, and glad his father was a nice man. But you broke a very important rule this morning. Take your friend to the river, and we'll talk tonight."

———

"I hope you don't get in too much trouble," Lil Mo said

to Martha Tom as they stood on the banks of the river.

"Oh, my mother wasn't really mad," said Martha Tom. "She'll warn me again and be fussy for a few days, that's all. Will you get in trouble, staying gone so long?"

"Maybe, but it was worth it," said Lil Mo. "You know why?"

"Why?" asked Martha Tom, already missing her new friend.

"I have never seen so many happy people, never in my life," said Lil Mo. "Everybody was happy. Nobody was afraid. Even your mother, Martha Tom. She was mad at you, but she was happy."

Martha Tom looked at the water, sparkling in the sunlight.

"Someday, Lil Mo, you will be happy. I know you will," she said.

CHAPTER 5

The Promised Land

Sunday morning, seven days later

Martha Tom woke up long before sunrise. She crawled out of bed, slipped on her clothes, and was tiptoeing out the door when her mother suddenly appeared.

"Where are you going and why are you sneaking around?" she asked.

"I didn't want to wake you up," Martha Tom said. "I'm going to pick corn for the bone pickers."

"Why are you going so early?"

"So they can start cooking early. They've been up for hours already."

"Hoke. Don't stay gone long."

"I might help them cook," Martha Tom said, grabbing

her basket and heading to the fields. She stooped and tossed and filled the basket with corn, but she didn't help the old women, the bone pickers, cook their breakfast.

No.

She dropped the basket at their door and walked as fast as she could to the river. She stepped across the stone walkway and hurried to the church of the field workers.

Lil Mo waved at her. "Come sit with my family," he said.

Martha Tom listened to the sermon and sang the songs. She loved their music, the way everyone sang together and apart at the same time. The men sang with deep voices while the women's voices floated and soared.

Martha Tom tried singing with a deep voice, like a man, just to see if she could.

"You sound like a growling dog," Lil Mo whispered, and she slapped his belly in reply.

"Bully!" he said.

"Mean boy!" she replied.

"Behave and be quiet," whispered Lil Mo's mother, while his father laughed and shook his head.

"How long does church last?" asked Martha Tom.

"Till around noon," Lil Mo answered.

"I better be going. My mother doesn't know where I am."

"I was wondering about that," said Lil Mo. "Can you find your way to the river?"

"Yes," said Martha Tom, "but a kind boy would walk with me anyway."

"I'll let you know if I see one," said Lil Mo. His mother and father looked at each other, then turned to Lil Mo and nodded their permission.

As he walked beside her, Martha Tom hummed the music to her newest favorite song.

"That's our calling song," said Lil Mo.

> *On Jordan's stormy banks we stand*
> *And cast a wishful eye*
> *To Canaan's fair and happy land*
> *Where our possessions lie.*
>
> *I am bound for the promised land,*
> *I am bound for the promised land,*
> *O, who will come and go with me?*
> *I am bound for the promised land.*

"What does the song mean?" asked Martha Tom.

"Remember what I was saying after the wedding? How nobody here is really happy? Everybody is always afraid of something—of somebody getting whipped or sold. Every day is full of hard work, but it's all for somebody else. We get nothing from our work."

"What kind of work do you do?" Martha Tom asked.

"Well, let's see," said Lil Mo, holding up his fingers and counting as he spoke. "I chase chickens. I pull weeds. I milk cows. And if somebody wants to hunt birds, who do you think drags the bloody dead birds from the bushes? Me, that's who. So we know, all of us, that this isn't our real home. We stand and look to the other shore, where we can be free."

"To the Choctaw side of the river?" asked Martha Tom.

"More like to heaven, to someplace where we can be happy."

"Would you be happy in Choctaw town?"

"I would never leave without my family. I would worry about my mother especially."

"What if your family could live in Choctaw town?" Martha Tom asked.

"Martha Tom, you better stop dreaming and hurry home," Lil Mo said. "I'll stay till you reach the other side."

———

Every Sunday for a month, Martha Tom sat with Lil Mo and his family at the field workers' church, and every Sunday she sang the song. As she crossed Bok Chitto River on her way home every week, she sang the song in English and Choctaw both.

Then trouble came.

CHAPTER 6

Stranger on a Dark Horse

Early one evening, after a long day of working in the fields, Lil Mo sat next to his younger sister Angel, like always, when suddenly Mr. Bledsoe appeared. Bledsoe was the overseer of the guards. He made certain they kept the slaves working, with no time to rest and no talking to each other. "Work!" he often shouted to the guards. "They are here to work."

Bledsoe was a cruel man who carried a bullwhip with him everywhere he went, and Lil Mo always did his best to avoid him—and now he stood in front of their house.

"Come out, Lavester!" he shouted.

Lavester, Lil Mo's father, jumped to his feet and stepped out the door. Bledsoe was surrounded by plantation guards, all on horseback and carrying shotguns.

Lavester knew these men, all but one. The stranger

was dressed like a wealthy man and sat on a black horse at Bledsoe's side.

"Yes. What is it?" Lavester asked.

"Bring your family and follow me," shouted Bledsoe. "Everyone. These men want to look at you all."

Bledsoe and his men rode from one house to another, knocking on doors and shouting. When the field workers and their families were gathered, the stranger dismounted from his horse. He walked first to Lil Mo's family, and finally stood before Lil Mo's mother. He lifted her chin and stuck his fingers inside her mouth.

"She has good teeth," he said, nodding to Bledsoe.

An hour later—after examining everyone by touching and poking—the man climbed onto his horse and rode away.

"All right, now," said Bledsoe. "I want the men to follow me. Everyone else go home and stay inside!"

Lavester and the other men walked behind Bledsoe. No one spoke. Some men cried, and others stiffened their jaws and fought back the tears. They knew where they were going.

The stranger was a slave trader. Soon he would stand before them while Bledsoe read the list. The people whose names he read would go with the slave trader.

They would never see their families again.

To Bledsoe, they were slaves.

To the fathers walking with their heads bowed, the names on the list were not slaves. They were wives and children and brothers and sisters. They were family.

The men feared this day even more than they feared Bledsoe's whip. The scars and cuts from Bledsoe's whip would someday heal. But the scars from the list would never heal. In ten short hours, the people whose names were on the list would be gone.

Forever.

CHAPTER 7

Last Meal Together

William Kendall, the plantation owner, met the group at the door of his house.

"Step inside," he said to the slave trader. "Come in and relax."

He then turned to Bledsoe, saying, "You, go to the porch and read the names. Let them know to be ready an hour before sunrise."

"Yes," said Bledsoe. "I understand."

Lavester watched through a window as Mr. Kendall and the slave trader settled on soft chairs by a fireplace. Cedar logs popped and glowed soft orange. A house servant appeared with a tray of iced drinks and snack cakes. The two men smiled while twenty feet away, outside, Bledsoe read the list aloud.

"Twenty slaves will be leaving for New Orleans tomorrow morning," he said in a loud voice. "The names I read will be ready an hour before sunrise. The guards will be at your door."

Lil Mo's mother was number seven on the list.

"Treda."

Lavester wanted to grab the list from Bledsoe's hand and rip it apart. But he did not.

He hung his head and began the longest walk of his life. As he stumbled through the dark woods on his way home, he whispered to himself, "My family will never be the same again, not after tonight. Not after I tell Treda."

As he stepped through the front door, Treda greeted him with a smile. She said nothing of the stranger who had stared at her.

"What took you so long?" she asked.

When he didn't answer, she kissed him on the cheek and led him to the table. "I have a surprise for you," she said.

Lil Mo rose and took the lid from a huge pot.

"Your favorite stew."

Lavester smelled the white bean stew, thick with floating onions and potatoes from the nearby garden. "Looks like supper is ready," he said, trying to smile.

"We were waiting on you," Lil Mo said.

I'll tell them after the meal, Lavester thought.

He ruffled Lil Mo's hair and blew a sweet kiss at Angel. No one spoke during the meal. When the last bite of beans was gone from bowl, Lavester stood behind Treda.

"Bledsoe read the names from the sale," he said. "The guards will come tomorrow morning, an hour before sunrise."

"Who was sold?" Treda asked. Lil Mo and Angel looked to their father and listened.

"Twenty people," said Lavester. "Twenty slaves will be moving to New Orleans."

"Who?"

Lavester turned away.

"People we know?" Treda asked.

"Yes."

"Who?"

Lavester said nothing.

"People we're close to?" asked Treda.

"Yes."

"Who?"

When Lavester didn't reply, she reached for his face and moved it close to hers. Tears were rising in his eyes.

"Just say it," Treda whispered. "Who?"

"You," he said, and the tears streamed down his face.

"No!" she said. She held his face tight between her palms and whispered, "I will not go. I won't leave you or the children."

"There's nothing we can do," he said. "It is a slave sale."

"I will *not* go!" shouted Treda, pushing Lavester away. "I will grab my clothes and run into the woods!"

Lil Mo and Angel began crying. They had never seen their parents act this way.

"You don't want the children to see the dogs drag you back," Lavester said. "You've seen that before. You don't want that to happen to you."

Treda looked to the children. They sobbed out loud. "Which of the children are going with us?" she asked.

"None of the children," said Lavester.

"How can they live without us?"

"Not us," said Lavester. "You. Only you."

Treda rocked back and forth, and her whole body shook.

My family is shattered, thought Lavester, *like broken glass*.

Treda stared at her children. Lavester knew she would always remember them this way, crying and afraid. He pounded his fist on the table.

"Stop your crying!" he shouted. "This is your last night with your mother. You will not see her again. I want every one of you to go to your corners. Find something small and precious to give to your mother to remember you by. You will not see her again."

No one moved.

"I am your father. Do what I say!"

This is all my fault, Lil Mo thought. It made no sense for Lil Mo to blame himself. But he did. *I have to make this right*. He pushed back his chair and stepped to his father's side.

"Papa," he said, "we can stay together. We can cross the river. The Choctaws will take us in."

"No, son," Lavester said. "It is a sale night. They'll be guarding the river."

"Please listen, Papa," said Lil Mo. His voice was soft but strong. "I know a secret crossing place. We can make it, just like you taught me. Remember? *Not too fast, not too slow, eyes to the ground, away we go.* We'll be invisible. We have to try."

Lavester looked at Lil Mo as if he were seeing him for the first time.

"You are right, son," he said. "We have to try."

CHAPTER 8

Running While Invisible

Lavester grabbed cloth from a stack by the door, cloth used to make carrying bundles. He turned to the children.

"Now run to your corners," he said. "Bring your clothes—only a few! Hurry! We may have to run. Go!"

The family sprang into action. They packed light and they packed quick.

But not quick enough. Bledsoe's guards were patrolling the houses while carrying lanterns and watching through the windows. When they saw Lil Mo's family scrambling and packing, they surrounded the house. Their shotguns were loaded and ready to fire.

Snarling dogs stood at their sides. The guards held their coats over the lanterns and waited in the shadows, unseen.

Inside the house Lil Mo and his family surrounded

Lavester, with their bundles over their shoulders, packed and ready to go.

"We could go out the back door," Lavester said. "It might be dark and safer that way. But this night is not about darkness and safety. This night is about faith and freedom. We will go out the front door."

And so they did, just as Lil Mo had reminded them.

"Not too fast, not too slow, eyes to the ground, away you go," he whispered.

Lavester pushed open the front door. The guards raised their shotguns. They had orders to fire at anyone trying to leave.

But they saw no one.

On a night that began as the worst nightmare of their lives, a miracle happened. As Lil Mo and his family walked out the door, the guards looked at one another and lowered their guns. They saw no one.

Lil Mo's family was *invisible*.

Lavester led his family down the steps, hurrying Lil Mo and Angel. As he turned to Treda and Angel, the guards threw their coats aside and held their lanterns high. The yard and the surrounding trees blazed with yellow beams of light.

Lavester froze. He expected Bledsoe to shout orders. He lifted his arms high and was about to shout, "Please don't shoot us! We'll do whatever you want."

Instead he lowered his arms in silence and was glad he did.

Bledsoe stepped to the front of the guards, as expected. But he said nothing. He did not shout orders to his men, as he always did. He grabbed a lantern from a guard and lifted it high, waving it back and forth as he approached the house.

He can't see us, Lavester thought, and his thought was shared by Lil Mo and his mother. The parents pulled the children close and gently put their hands over their mouths to keep them quiet.

Bledsoe walked within a few feet of where Lavester and his family waited. He walked past Treda and the children as if they were not there.

"Did anyone see who opened the door?" Bledsoe asked. "Check the back door. Maybe they ran out that way. Check inside the house!"

Lavester held his breath and hoped his family knew to be quiet, very quiet. Their lives depended on silence.

Lil Mo quickly realized what had happened. *We are invisible,* he thought. *I knew it!*

He held Angel tight and felt for his mother. As if they had planned the escape and knew what to do, everyone waited while Lavester tapped heads and counted.

Treda, Angel, and Lil Mo.

Lavester placed Treda's hand on his shoulder. He took

Lil Mo and Angel by the wrist, and then slowly and quietly, they walked across the dirt road, through a small grove of pines, and into the cotton fields. When they were well out of sight, Lavester knelt and huddled everyone together.

"Can anyone see me?" he asked.

"No," everyone whispered at once.

"Lil Mo, I guess we have been chosen for something very special," he said. "But the dogs are trained to catch escaped slaves. They can still sniff us out. We need to hurry. You take the lead, son. If anyone falls or loses touch, don't holler. Just whisper and let us know where you are. Now, let's go!"

Behind them, Bledsoe shouted louder and louder. "What do you mean, you can't find them?" His voice rang across the fields. He popped his whip. "Check every-where in the house!"

He grabbed a shotgun from a guard and fired it through the front door.

Boom!

"Come out, or you'll all die!" he shouted.

"Keep going," said Lavester. "Hurry." As they reached the river, the sky lit up. Men shouted, and more shotgun blasts shook the air.

"Wait," said Lavester. "Take one last look at what we are leaving behind." Red-and-blue flames leapt and twisted, boards crashed and fell, and bright yellow embers rose like fireflies in the night.

"He's burning down the house," Treda said. "He would have killed us all."

For a brief moment the family watched. "When we turn our backs and cross the river, we are leaving our home," Lavester said. "But we are also leaving Bledsoe, his whip, and the fires and dogs of darkness. Remember that, and know that I love you all."

He turned to Lil Mo. "You saved us once tonight," he said. "Now, take us to the crossing path."

The family soon stood on the muddy banks of the river Bok Chitto. Fog rose from the banks, and the moonlight played on the waters. His family waited as Lil Mo stepped along the shoreline. Everyone listened to the sloshing lift and fall of his steps. Back and forth Lil Mo walked.

"Son?" asked Lavester.

"Papa, I'm sorry," said Lil Mo. "I've never been here at night, and the fog isn't helping. I can't find the path!"

Lavester grabbed Lil Mo by the waist and held him close till their faces touched. "Son," he said, "we call you Lil Mo. But you know that's not your real name. I know now why we named you Moses. Now, Moses, get us across that river!"

CHAPTER 9

Bound for the Promised Land

Lil Mo leapt from his father's arms and ran to the river. He fell to his knees and stuck his palms in the muddy water. Up and down the riverbank he crawled, till he found the stone pathway.

"I'll get help!" he whispered. "Wait here."

He ran from stone to stone and jumped over the last two. Landing on the shore, he dashed to Martha Tom's house.

"Help!" he called out, knocking on the door. "It's me, Lil Mo. Please help me!"

Martha Tom's mother flung a window curtain aside. "What is it, Lil Mo?"

"My mother has been sold, and we're coming over. The men with the dogs and guns are after us. Can you help?"

"Get yourself right back across that river," she said,

climbing out of bed. "Hide your family in the tall river cane. The fog will help hide you. Go now! I have work to do. You'll know when to cross. Go!"

A shotgun blast split the silence.

"Are you there?" she asked. "Where are you, Lil Mo? I can't see you!"

"No time to explain!" he shouted over his shoulder as he ran to the river. He soon reached the shore, took a deep breath, and jumped onto the stone path.

As he neared the plantation shore, he felt himself slipping. He waved his arms and fell forward. His father heard the splash and caught him just before he sank, then dragged him to the bank.

"Papa," said Lil Mo, "I'm glad you were there."

"Will the Choctaws help us?" Lavester asked.

"Yes. Martha Tom's mother is coming. She said for us to hide in the river cane till she gets here."

Lil Mo turned his father's head to a patch of cane growing in the water and stretching to the shore. "There!"

Lavester and Lil Mo dove into the cane, slapping thick stalks aside. When they reached the muddy shoreline, they broke the stalks, forming a small circle.

"This way, Treda. Bring the girls," Lavester whispered. Soon everyone sat clinging to each other, waiting.

The lantern light was lost in the flames of their burning house, so no one saw the men approaching. By the time they heard the dogs bark, the guards stood a few feet away. Bledsoe was not among them. Treda shivered and pulled her children closer.

"Shhh," Lavester said. He took off his shirt, which was dripping with sweat. He wadded it into a tight ball so it wouldn't be seen, and tossed it at a low-hanging tree branch twenty feet away. The dogs growled and leapt after the smell of the shirt, dancing around the base of the tree.

"There!" shouted a guard. The others held the lanterns high.

"Come down, or we'll shoot you down!" shouted Harold, a young guard.

"Wait. Let's give them a chance to climb down," said an older guard.

That's Mr. Porter, thought Lil Mo. Mr. Porter was a guard, one who watched over the slaves in the fields, but he was never as mean as the other guards. He never carried a whip. He never beat the older slaves, like Bledsoe often did.

Treda pulled Lil Mo close, as if she read his thoughts. She knew Mr. Porter, too.

"There's no one there," said Mr. Porter. "Zeke, climb up and make sure. Someone help him." Harold, looking grumpy at being roped into helping, leaned against the tree, and Zeke stood on his shoulders, reaching for the first branch.

With the guards searching through the pines for the runaways, Martha Tom and her mother had all the time they needed. They ran from house to house in Choctaw town, knocking on doors and calling through windows.

"Wake up!" they shouted. "Women, we need you now! No time to talk. Hurry! Bring candles and meet us at the river crossing!"

Soon Martha Tom and Ella, her mother, led thirty Choctaw women from their homes. They crossed acres of cornfields, quick-stepping through the woods, till finally they stood on the foggy banks of the river Bok Chitto.

"Now," Ella said, "light your candles. Hide them with your hands at first. We want a soft yellow glow. That's all we want them to see." The Choctaw women lit their candles and covered them with their palms.

"Look yonder, look at that!" a guard shouted, pointing to the Choctaw side. The fog was thick, but the shore was alive with flickering circles of light.

Slow as a dream, the fog lifted just enough for the guards to see. Choctaw women carrying candles were floating on the riverbank like angels. They held the candles high, and yellow light circled their faces like haloes.

Lavester stood up first. As everyone stood to join him, something unexpected happened. A shivering light surrounded the family. For the first time since they left home, they could see each other.

"We are not invisible anymore," said Lil Mo.

The guards lifted their rifles and aimed at Lil Mo's family, ready to fire. But their fingers froze on the triggers, for stepping from the fog on the Choctaw side came Martha Tom. She walked on the water without looking at her feet, unafraid of falling. The moonlight sparkled on the river and the fog hung heavy.

One unseen stone at a time came Martha Tom. The guards pointed their guns at her. Lil Mo almost cried out for them to stop, but Lavester gripped his shoulder.

"Time to wait and watch, son," he whispered.

Martha Tom reached out her hand as she walked. The guards held their shotguns to their shoulders, staring at the miracle of this candlelit angel who walked on the water. As if the night were not magic enough, Martha Tom began to sing.

She sang the song in Choctaw, and the family shivered to hear it. It was the calling song. The women hummed while Martha Tom sang.

> *Nitak ishtayo pickmano,*
> *Chisus-ut minitit,*
> *Umala Holitopama,*
> *Chohot ayalaski.*
>
> *I am bound for the promised land,*

44

I am bound for the promised land,
O, who will come and go with me?
I am bound for the promised land.

Mr. Porter dropped his shotgun, and the others soon followed. One by one they fell to their knees on the muddy banks of the river Bok Chitto.

Martha Tom took Lil Mo by the hand, and he turned to his mother, reaching for her outstretched hand. Lavester held tight to Angel, and together they crossed the river, step by careful step. When his feet finally touched the soil of Choctaw land, Lil Mo gave one final look across the river. He thought he saw Joseph, his secret friend Joseph—the son of Mr. Porter—hiding in the bushes.

As the family disappeared in the fog on the Choctaw side, Martha Tom blew out her candle, and so did the older women. Lil Mo and his family stood in the moonlight, hidden by the fog from the guards and their guns, surrounded and protected by Choctaw women.

CHAPTER 10

Lil Mo's New Friends

1808, Bok Chitto, Choctaw Nation

The Choctaw women led Lil Mo and his family through the main street of Choctaw town, past homes and gardens and into the woods.

"Balili!" they shouted. They wrapped a blanket around every member of the family.

"Balili!"

The moon disappeared, and pine trees grew so close together their limbs entwined.

"Now, time to rest," said Ella, Martha Tom's mother. Huffing from the long run, Lil Mo's family sat on the soft pine needles of the forest floor.

"The men will keep watch. Nothing will happen till

morning. Stay here till then and keep away from the river," she said.

Exhausted, Lil Mo and his family soon fell asleep. As he closed his eyes, Lil Mo heard his mother crying softly. He knew his father held her close. His father's voice was the real blanket, covering everyone with hopeful words.

"Watch over us and deliver us from evil," Lavester whispered.

Two hours before sunrise, Lil Mo rolled over and felt a broken tree limb stab him in the stomach. "Owwww!" he called out. He knew he should be quiet, but it hurt too much. He couldn't help it.

"Shhhh!"

He rolled backward and another branch stabbed him in the ribs.

"Owwww!"

"Shhhh!"

Lil Mo stared at the moon and the winking stars. He thought his leg itched, but he was wrong. His leg was a mountain range. Twenty ants climbed the mountains, from his ankle to his knee, in search of food.

They found no food, so they dug into his leg. When Lil Mo scratched where they dug, the ants did what ants do: They stung. Twenty angry ants stung Lil Mo's leg at the same time.

"Owwww!"

"Shhhh!"

Lil Mo jumped up and pulled off his pants. He brushed away the ants from his ankles to his waist.

"Shhhh!"

He shook his pants till he was certain every ant was gone. He felt like crying. *Plenty to cry about,* he thought, *but too much to be thankful for to cry over a few puny ants.*

As if she understood, a momma ant sank her fangs deep into Lil Mo's calf.

"Owwww!"

"Shhhh!"

Lil Mo moved away from the camp and headed to the riverbank. The bites still stung, but the night sky held a stronger pull. The fog had lifted, and thin threads of flying clouds passed over the moon. Lil Mo sat on a rock and watched the river sparkle.

He didn't notice when the moonlight shifted from white to a soft green glow. He closed his eyes and hung his head for a few moments of sleep. When he woke up, the green glow was everywhere, and the air hummed.

And Lil Mo was no longer alone.

Four men sat close to him, surrounding the rock. Later he wondered why he didn't jump up and run. But everything seemed so peaceful and normal.

The men were neither nahullos nor dark-skinned like himself. They appeared to be tiny Choctaws, barely waist high to Lil Mo. They wore long britches with no shirts and sat in a circle around a campfire.

One man stirred a sweet-smelling brew in a pot. Another carved a branch with a deer-bone knife. A third clacked together stones, while the last one twisted vines, weaving a long, thin rope.

Though they ignored him, Lil Mo had the feeling these men wanted to be seen. They wanted him to know they were there. The fire glowed green, and so did the air around them.

Suddenly the men looked to the sky across the river. Lil Mo followed their gaze. He heard the sharp call of a shrieking owl. "O-hooo! O-hooo!" A cold wind shook the trees, and Lil Mo shivered.

The men scrambled to their feet. The fire disappeared, and all was cloaked in darkness. Lil Mo stood to go, but his feet flew out from under him. He tumbled to the rocks and slipped into the water.

He waved his arms and fought to keep from sinking, but deeper and deeper into the river he fell. Through a thin veil of water Lil Mo saw a lantern, hanging from the end of a long tree branch. Someone from the plantation shore was trying to see to the other side.

Whoever held the branch swung the lantern over the water. The lantern moved slowly. The beam of light crept like evil footprints over the water, from stone to stone, one step at a time.

Lil Mo knew that the man who held the lantern also held a shotgun. Maybe several men watched and waited for a target. He was too scared to move. He held his breath underwater and waited for the light to go away. For what seemed like hours he waited, without breathing. His lungs grew hot, and his cheeks swelled.

Finally, the light moved away. Lil Mo let himself drift to the surface. Just before he burst from the water, a face appeared above him. The lantern shone bright in his eyes, and Harold, the bullying sixteen-year-old white boy from the plantation, glared down at him, hanging from the side of a boat. His eyes were fired by hatred, and he reached through the water for Lil Mo's neck. He dug his fingers deep into Lil Mo's throat and squeezed hard.

"Owwww!"

Lil Mo kicked his legs and tried to swim away. He grabbed Harold's hands and tried to free himself, but Harold was stronger. Lil Mo felt the blood pounding in his head. His eyes bulged from their sockets.

Suddenly, Harold was gone. A Choctaw boy lifted Lil Mo from the water. He was Lil Mo's age, and black hair hung over his shoulders. He wore a white shirt, and a turtle-shell necklace dangled from a string around his neck.

"You saved my life," said Lil Mo. "Thank you. What is your name?"

The boy opened his mouth and spoke, but Lil Mo heard nothing.

"What?"

Once more the boy moved his lips, but no sound came out.

"What?" said Lil Mo. "Speak louder!"

"Shhhh!"

Lil Mo opened his eyes. His legs still stung, but he lay wrapped in his blanket, surrounded by his family. The green glow and the tiny men were gone.

Harold and the Choctaw boy were nowhere to be seen. Lil Mo felt his clothes. They were dry. He jumped to his feet.

"Where is the Choctaw boy who saved me?" he asked.

Angel shrugged. "You were having a bad dream," she said. "Nobody else is here."

"Everything seemed so real," he said. But she was right. They weren't anywhere near the river. He wouldn't have gone back to the riverside, where he knew he could be seen by the plantation guards. Would he?

"You're safe now, son," said Lavester. "Go back to sleep. Tomorrow will be a busy day."

51

"I'm sorry I woke everybody up," said Lil Mo. As he lay back down, he knew he had passed through a door into a new world—a Choctaw world. He knew he had four small friends and one Choctaw boy who would be there when he needed them.

He also knew he had at least one powerful enemy, Harold. Lil Mo expected to hear the owl again. A shiver passed through him, and he knew he would never be free of the owl.

"I must stay on guard. Always. Our lives depend on this," he told himself.

CHAPTER 11

Lil Mo's Family on the Freedom Side

1808, Bok Chitto, Choctaw Nation

In a few hours the sun rose on Lil Mo's first day in Choctaw town, and he woke up to the smell of cooking meat.

"That smells good, Papa. What is it?"

His father and an old Choctaw man held sticks over the morning fire, cooking small chunks of meat. Hot juices dripped into the flames, and the meat smoked and sizzled.

"I'll help," Lil Mo said.

The Choctaw man handed him a stick of meat.

"You must be Lil Mo," he said.

"Yes. Who are you?"

"My name is Funi Man," he said, "and the meat is squirrel."

"Why do they call you Funi Man?"

"Funi means 'squirrel' in Choctaw talk," said Funi Man. "I am a good squirrel hunter, so that's what they named me."

Funi Man is a really funny name, thought Lil Mo. *I wonder if he's just a good squirrel hunter, or if he's funny, too. I hope he's funny.*

Funi Man looked at Lil Mo as if he knew what he was thinking.

"I bet you can climb trees and hide behind leaves," Funi Man said.

"Sometimes," said Lil Mo.

"That's what I thought," said Funi Man, reaching for his blow-dart gun. "Maybe you're the real squirrel here. Don't move. You can be our supper."

"No!" yelled Lil Mo, laughing at Funi Man's joke.

"Why not?" said Funi Man.

"You don't want to cook me! I just got here."

"You're right," said Funi Man. "You need to grow some. When you have more meat on your bones, then we'll cook you."

Lil Mo smiled. *I have another friend,* he thought.

The squirrel meat was delicious. Ella, Martha Tom's mother, arrived after breakfast with a basketful of blackberries.

"For a few days you can all stay here," she said. "We surrounded your camp with watchers last night." She turned to a thick clump of bushes. "Come out, Koi Losa. I want them to meet you."

The Choctaw boy from Lil Mo's dream appeared.

"This is Koi Losa. 'Black Panther' in Choctaw talk. He is one of your watchers."

"Halito. Hello," said Koi Losa.

Lil Mo stared at him, wondering if he knew of the dream. Koi Losa even wore the turtleshell necklace, just like in the dream, but he looked at Lil Mo as if he were seeing him for the first time.

I guess not, thought Lil Mo.

"Koi Losa will always be close," said Ella. "You won't see him. But if the men from the plantation come, he'll take you to safety."

"Good to meet you," said Lil Mo's father. "My name is Lavester. This is my wife, Treda." One by one the rest of the family rose and greeted their watcher.

"We're thankful you are here," said Treda. She spoke softly, and her eyes were red from crying.

"Today it's best if you stay here," said Funi Man. "I'll bring people to meet you. We are glad you're here."

"You are all welcome here," said Martha Tom's mother. "And my name is Ella, so everybody call me that."

"Thank you," said Treda. For the first time in two

days, a smile crept across her face. "It's good to be here, Ella. You must be very proud of Martha Tom. You have a brave daughter."

"Thank you," said Ella, "and you have a brave son."

"Maybe Lil Mo can help Koi Losa," said Funi Man.

"I want to help him!" Lil Mo said. "What can I do?"

"You can help him watch over the camp," said Funi Man. "He will show you how to hide and keep a sharp eye out for everything that moves."

Koi Losa looked at Lil Mo, studying him. "Let's go," he finally said. Lil Mo followed him into the thick grove of trees.

"I heard you say you could climb trees," Koi Losa said. "That's good. You'll make a good watcher."

Lil Mo and Koi Losa spent the day climbing oak trees and hiding behind clumps of leaves. Once Koi Losa pointed to the nearby river, then to his eyes.

He talks with his hands, thought Lil Mo.

By early afternoon Ella appeared with enough food for everyone. Bread and corn were spread out on a blanket, and soon every member of Lil Mo's family feasted on this new—at least to Lil Mo's family *new*—and delicious food.

Everyone except Lil Mo.

He looked at Koi Losa to see what they should do. Koi Losa held up a palm.

Wait.

Ella carried a basket of food to the foot of the tree and sat down as if she were about to eat. In a few minutes she joined the others by the fire, leaving the basket.

Koi Losa pointed to the basket. He pointed to Lil Mo, then to himself.

That is for us.

Koi Losa crept slowly to the end of a tree limb. Almost before Lil Mo realized he was gone, Koi Losa reappeared with the basket, wrapping his legs around the tree limb and motioning for Lil Mo to join him. The two boys dove into the food.

He hasn't eaten since yesterday, thought Lil Mo. *He's a good friend, to go without eating just to watch over us.*

The day moved slowly for Lil Mo's family, but for Lil Mo it was a day of learning.

To Koi Losa, *everything* was important. If a bird chirped, there was a reason. Maybe the reason was somebody crossing the river. If a branch snapped, there was a reason. Maybe the reason was someone sneaking close to the camp.

He not only heard and saw everything, Koi Losa also investigated everything.

Lil Mo could barely keep up with his friend. Koi Losa slid down the tree trunk, he flew across the ground to the riverbank, he darted in and out of trees and bushes with such speed Lil Mo stopped trying to chase him.

Once, when he lost sight of Koi Losa, Lil Mo stretched his neck and squinted. He peered through tall stalks of river cane, but couldn't find him. He turned away from the river.

He'll come back when he's ready, he thought. He took two steps, and Koi Losa jumped from a tree limb, landing on his feet in front of Lil Mo.

"Hey!" Lil Mo shouted. "Don't do that. I'm just learning my way around here."

"Sorry," said Koi Losa. "I just wanted to show you how to get around. No need to keep your feet on the ground."

"Yeah," said Lil Mo. "I can see that."

While Lil Mo and Koi Losa were climbing and exploring, the men built a lean-to for Lil Mo's family. They wove pine and cedar branches together to make a roof, and leaned the roof against the trunk of a large tree. It was a small room, with the tree trunk forming the back wall.

As they circled the lean-to, Koi Losa held up his hand. "Wait," he whispered. "Nahullos are near. Stay hidden."

Koi Losa climbed a cypress tree and motioned for Lil Mo to move to the bushes. Lil Mo understood. If an enemy was in the camp, he was probably looking for Lil Mo's family.

"Caw! Caw! Caw!" A crow's call came from the cypress

tree. Lil Mo looked up, expecting a bird to fly from the treetop. Nothing moved. Not a single leaf stirred.

That must be Koi Losa, calling a warning!

"Caw! Caw! Caw!"

Funi Man stepped from the lean-to with his rifle, cocked and ready for shooting.

CHAPTER 12

Better Run, Harold

As soon as Funi Man stepped into view, they heard a sudden rustling and breaking of branches. Somebody was running to the river!

"I know him. That's Harold," Lil Mo said.

Harold's face was red, and his arms were pumping. Lil Mo wanted to cheer. He wanted to grab a branch and chase Harold into the river.

"Let's see how fast you can swim!" he wanted to shout.

But something told him to wait. He was not the leader today. Koi Losa jumped from the tree and motioned for Lil Mo to follow. They stayed behind Harold.

Why are we doing this? Lil Mo thought. *We can outrun Harold. He's big and slow.*

When Harold pulled a boat from a hiding place on the Choctaw side, Lil Mo understood. *Koi Losa wants to know how Harold crossed the river, and where he hid his boat. Good to know for the future.*

Harold paddled quickly to the plantation side, and as the boys walked back to the lean-to, Koi Losa spoke.

"He never saw you, Lil Mo. Since Funi Man scared him away, and not your father, he never saw any of your family. That's good. He can't report back that your family is still in Choctaw town. I'm sure that's why they sent him. And you know him?"

"Yes. His name is Harold, and he's a friend of Joseph's. But he's not the kind of friend you can ever trust."

"Who is Joseph?"

"He was my best friend."

"Maybe someday he and his family can cross over, too," said Koi Losa.

"That will never happen," said Lil Mo.

"Why not?"

"His father's a guard. He and his men chased us to the river."

"Your best friend is the son of a slave guard?" Koi Losa asked.

"Yes," said Lil Mo.

"And you trust him? How do you know he didn't tell somebody about your plans to cross?"

"Joseph knew nothing about our plans to cross the river," said Lil Mo. "And yes, I trust him. He's been my best friend since we were little kids. We had to hide our friendship. Nobody knows, not even my family."

"That's how you learned to move and hide in the woods," said Koi Losa.

"Yes," said Lil Mo. "I also learned to be very careful about who you can trust and who you can't."

"So who are Harold's friends? Will they cause trouble?"

"Yes. They are the meanest people I have ever met. They won't give up trying to get us back. Bledsoe is the worst. He likes to use his whip."

"I've heard about whips and beatings, but never seen anything like that. Have you?" asked Koi Losa.

"Yes." Lil Mo nodded. "That's why we are all so happy to be here."

"We are happy, too," Koi Losa said, "and every Choctaw in town will keep you safe."

"Thank you," said Lil Mo.

"Yakoke," said Koi Losa. "Learn to say yakoke. That is 'thank you' in Choctaw."

"Yakoke," said Lil Mo. He smiled, realizing he had just spoken his first Choctaw word. "Yakoke," he repeated. He liked the sound of saying "thank you" in Choctaw.

CHAPTER 13

Mr. Porter Goes to Jail

The day following the crossing, plantation side

Soon after Lil Mo and his family disappeared into the fog, the guards returned to their homes. They lived with their families in small wooden homes half a mile from the plantation house. Knowing their story would never be believed, the guards were afraid to report to work the next day. Long before sunrise, they gathered at the home of Sam Porter, the head guard who worked under Mr. Bledsoe.

"What are we gonna tell Bledsoe?" asked Zeke, Sam Porter's elder son and also a guard. He was old enough that he didn't live in the house with Joseph and their mother and father anymore. "Nobody will believe us if we say that slave family walked across the river."

Bledsoe supervised the guards and eyed their every move. He was a thin man with a violent temper—and his cruelty with the whip was known to all.

"That's what we saw," said Mr. Porter. "All of 'em, walking on the river."

"I don't care what we saw, and neither will Bledsoe. He'll start cracking his whip and won't stop till every one of us gets it!"

"Anybody else would have done the same thing," said Mr. Porter. "That Choctaw girl was singing a hymn. Last night was like being in church, right there on the riverbank."

"Try convincing Bledsoe. We'll be lucky if we're not picking cotton."

"He's trusted me for years," said Mr. Porter. "I'll tell him I gave the order to drop your guns."

"You must be crazy. You know what kinda temper he has."

"Better he take his anger out on an old friend," said Mr. Porter, "than young men he hardly knows."

Mr. Porter was almost fifty, but stooped like a man much older. His hair was thick and already gray. He had been kicked in the leg by a stubborn mule when he was barely twenty, and his right knee had never been the same after that.

While the guards argued about what to tell Bledsoe, Joseph rolled out of bed. He carried his bowl of oatmeal to the porch and sat down to listen. His mother stood by the window, in easy earshot of all that was said.

When Mrs. Porter heard her husband say he would take the blame for losing the slaves, she shook her head and wrapped her arms tightly around herself. Mr. Porter would protect everyone else first, without worrying about what Bledsoe might do to punish him. More than once he had spent the night at a friend's house rather than let his wife see the fresh cuts from Bledsoe's whip. But she knew. She always knew.

"Well, we best not be late today," said Mr. Porter, emptying his coffee cup and rising slowly. "Joseph," he called out, "help your mother wash these cups and tell her I'll see her this evening."

That was the last thing Sam Porter said to his family before he entered the darkest days of his life.

When he did not return home at the usual evening hour, Mrs. Porter grew nervous. "Joseph," she finally said, "run to the barn and see how long your father will be."

"Yes, ma'am," Joseph replied, and stepped from the porch. "Reddog!" he hollered, and his golden retriever joined him on his dash. Joseph smiled to see how she struggled to keep up with him. "The puppies must be growing inside her belly," he said, and slowed his pace.

Twenty running steps from the barn, Joseph grabbed the trunk of a tree and pulled himself to a stop. "Reddog," he whispered, "come here."

Reddog snuggled against him, and Joseph rubbed her ears. "Shhh, girl," he said. "Let's stay here and watch." This late in the evening, the barn was usually empty, but a man holding a lantern lingered in the doorway.

"How long you think you'll be here?" It was the voice of his oldest brother, Zeke. Joseph strained to hear, but whoever replied spoke in a whisper.

"Can we do anything to help?" asked Zeke. Silence again, while someone spoke quietly. Zeke said, "I can't leave you here without knowing how long before he lets you out. You are my father."

Joseph hoped he had misheard Zeke. "Why would Dad spend the night in the barn?" he asked himself.

He crept to the rear of the barn and peered through the cracks in the wall. He knew there was a jail in the barn, where slaves were kept when they first arrived. If a slave made Bledsoe angry, he would be whipped and thrown in the jail for sometimes a week. But Joseph had never heard of a *white* person in this jail.

Zeke now stood before the jail. It was a small cell in the corner of the barn, with two walls of iron bars. The floor was caked in sawdust, and a thick iron chain snaked across the floor.

Joseph shuddered. The chain was wrapped around his father's right ankle. Now he was close enough to hear his father speak.

"Zeke, be very careful," Mr. Porter said. "I have never seen Bledsoe so mad. I am lucky to be alive. Maybe come see me every few days. Wait till after dark and make sure no one else is here. If you can, bring me something to eat."

"I'll bring you supper every night," said Zeke. "What should I tell Mother?"

"Tell her Bledsoe needed more field workers. Say I went on a slave-buying trip. Tell her I'll be gone for two weeks, maybe a month. Tell your mother I had to leave today and tell her not to worry."

"I don't like leaving you here," said Zeke.

"There is nothing you can do," Mr. Porter said. "Be careful. Bledsoe will be looking hard at you, just waiting for you to cross him. Stay safe, and I'll soon be out."

CHAPTER 14

The Painful Truth

Half an hour later Zeke reported to his mother. Mrs. Porter listened patiently.

"Dad wants Joseph and me to take care of you while he's on the buying trip," Zeke said. "I'll drop by every evening and make sure you have everything you need."

"Where is he and how long did he say he would be gone?" she asked over and over, each time studying Zeke with a watchful eye.

Joseph pretended to be asleep through this conversation, but he heard every word. *Mother doesn't believe him*, he thought.

Zeke shuffled nervously, till finally Mrs. Porter said, "Nothing could be worse than what I'm imagining. Please tell me the truth. I am stronger than you or your father know. Tell me the truth."

Joseph lifted himself from his bed and slipped beside her chair. The silence hung thick, like smoke from a clogged chimney. Zeke lowered his head.

"He's in the barn," he whispered.

"The barn? You mean, Bledsoe had him jailed?"

Zeke said nothing.

"For how long?"

"No one knows. I was afraid to ask."

"I said I could take the truth," she said. "I can. I want you to watch the barn every hour, day and night. From a distance, from the woods, however you do it. Never let your father out of your hearing, if not your sight. Can you promise me this?"

Zeke nodded. Joseph nodded too, and when his mother saw this, she touched him on the shoulder.

"I can reshoe the mules in the corral by the barn," Zeke said. "They've been needing new shoes. I can do it after the fieldwork, and that way I can stay close to Dad."

He walked out the back door and Joseph hugged his mother. "Good night, Mother," he said, "and don't forget, Dad is strong. He'll be home soon."

Long after his mother went to sleep, Joseph climbed out of bed, dipped the ladle into the bucket on the porch, and carried a cup of cool water to his father. The woods were thick between his house and the barn, but he dared not take the road. Reddog followed, creeping quiet and close to the ground.

When they reached the barn, Joseph turned to Reddog. "Stay," he whispered, and Reddog sat on her hindquarters, ready to leap if needed. Joseph eased the door open and made his way to the rear of the barn. "Dad," he said, "I brought you some water."

His father took the cup and nodded his thanks without speaking. His face was bruised and purple, and his eyes were swollen shut. He tossed the water down his throat in one coughing swallow, spilling half of it.

"Careful, Dad," Joseph said. He stooped to his father and, reaching through the bars, wiped the water from his face with his shirt. Very slowly, Mr. Porter opened one eye. He spread it apart with a finger and a thumb, wincing as he did so.

"Thank you, Joseph," he said. "I worry about you more than your brother."

"Why?" asked Joseph.

"You are the most like me," his father said.

"I like hearing you say that. I want to be like you."

"Caring too much can be dangerous, Joseph." He stared at Joseph with his one open eye. "Look what happened to me."

Joseph wanted to comfort his father, but the words froze in his throat. He wanted to tell his father about Lil

Mo and his family, about the good people his father had saved. But no words came.

"Did I hear Reddog outside?" Mr. Porter asked. Joseph nodded. "Is she getting fat yet?"

"No," said Joseph, "not too fat. She can still run."

"Her puppies should be coming any day now, I'm thinking. By the next full moon, Reddog should be giving birth."

"Dad, that's great," Joseph said.

His father nodded and leaned his head against the wall. "Take care of her, son. Before all of this happened, I had plans for one of the pups."

"What plans, Dad?"

"I wanted you to give the firstborn pup to your best friend."

Joseph stepped back in surprise. He could not believe what he was hearing.

"My best friend?" he stammered, hanging his head and avoiding his father's eyes.

"Yes, Joseph, your best friend. Lil Mo."

"Dad! You know about me and Lil Mo?"

"I've known about your friendship for years, son. I'm proud of you for it. I'm also proud that you've been smart enough to keep it a secret."

"Does Mother know?"

"Yes. You know your mother keeps an eye on you."

"But Dad, why didn't you fuss at me, or something?"

"Joseph, we didn't see any harm in it. We still don't."

CHAPTER 15

Laws and Lawbreakers

1808, second night in Choctaw town

Inside the lean-to, the evening fire burned low. Ashes glowed yellow-red, and a smoky smell filled the room. Ella brought another basket of food—corn, fresh-picked river grapes, and bread. Martha Tom followed behind her mother, carrying a bowl of thick corn soup.

"This is pashofa," Martha Tom announced. "I cracked the corn and cooked it all by myself. Here, Lil Mo, you take the first bite." She dipped a spoon into the bowl and handed it to Lil Mo.

"Mmm, I bet it's good," he said.

Everyone waited. Lil Mo made a face and stuck out his tongue.

"What?" said Martha Tom. "I tasted it. It's good pashofa!"

"Of course," said Lil Mo. "That's the face I always make when something is really good!"

"That's not funny," said Martha Tom.

"I think it was kinda funny," said Funi Man. "Not really funny, but funny for a little kid." Everyone laughed, and he beamed.

"Your family should stay in the lean-to for a while," Ella said to Lavester. "The boys will keep watch. Stay close to the lean-to, and you'll be safe."

"That will be fine," said Lavester. "Thank you."

"You should know," Ella continued with a grave tone in her voice, "the trouble from your crossing will not go away. The plantation people will do everything to bring you back. Be very careful and stay away from the river."

"Yes," said Lavester. "We know."

"The Choctaw council is not simply waiting for Bledsoe and his men to attack," said Ella.

"You know about Bledsoe?" asked Lavester.

"Yes, we have known about him for years. He wants us gone. He and the plantation owners want our land."

"Who protects you?" he asked.

"We are well armed, and the law protects us. We are our own nation. We signed a treaty with the United States. On this side of the river, our Choctaw laws are followed."

"What about us?" Lavester asked.

"As long as you are with us, Bledsoe can do nothing, not legally. You are protected by Choctaw law."

"What will happen?"

"We expect Bledsoe to cross the river. He does not respect the law. For now, we must be careful. We watch everything that happens. We wait."

Lil Mo saw worried looks pass from face to face around the lean-to.

"We are not an army," Ella said, "but we have several men with guns. They know how to use them, and they will protect you. When you are with Choctaws, you are safe."

"Caw, caw!" The cry came from close overhead.

Funi Man rose to go. "Stay here for now," he said to Lil Mo. "There was no warning in that call."

Everyone waited in silence. In two minutes Funi Man returned. "Hoke, Lil Mo," he said, "your turn to watch. Koi Losa will show you where. Are you ready?"

"Yes, I am," said Lil Mo. "I got us into this trouble, and I need to get us out of it."

Funi Man slapped Lil Mo on the shoulder and said, "Yes, little one, you sure are a troublemaker! Now, go take your turn and let Koi Losa get some food!"

Everyone laughed. Lil Mo left the warm fire to take his place among the bushes surrounding the lean-to. Koi

Losa stepped from the shadows and nodded to Lil Mo. He pointed to a tall oak tree, thick with foliage.

"The limbs are low. The tree is easy to climb. You can see the river and the lean-to from there, and Choctaw town, too. It's a good place to watch."

"Yakoke," said Lil Mo.

"Just call if you see anything."

"Caw, caw!" Lil Mo yelled, practicing. Koi Losa nodded, hiding his smile from his newest friend, and ducked into the lean-to.

Lil Mo circled the tree. A small log had been rolled against it. He stepped onto the log and hoisted himself onto the lowest tree branch. From his perch, he watched the fog hanging over Bok Chitto.

Any real danger will come from the river, he thought. *So, Bledsoe is already well known by the Choctaws.*

As he watched the moonlight play on the slow-moving waters, Lil Mo thought of Bledsoe. *Why are people the way they are?* Lil Mo had once seen Bledsoe crack his whip on the back of an old man who moved too slow for his liking. *The man was the oldest worker in the fields*, thought Lil Mo. *How could anybody hurt an old man?*

Lil Mo also knew he had to guard his secret friendship. *Maybe Koi Losa can watch for me while I talk to Joseph.*

A sudden flash of light on the water jerked him from his thinking. He sat up and saw a torchlight approaching the river. Six guards settled on the plantation side. One of the guards was Zeke, Mr. Porter's oldest son and Joseph's brother.

For the next half hour Lil Mo watched as they built a fire, surrounded by a circle of stones. The men sat close to the fire. They boiled water for coffee and spoke quietly. One man—his shotgun held close—stayed awake as a night watchman, while the others unrolled their blankets and settled into sleep.

They are guarding the river, Lil Mo thought, *just like us*. He took a long, deep breath. *Not good. A fight is brewing.*

CHAPTER 16

Funi Man the Teacher

Lil Mo considered calling out, cawing a warning, then decided against it. Instead, he slid down the tree trunk and stuck his head in the lean-to.

"Funi Man," he whispered. "Something you should see here." Funi Man stepped quietly behind him, and Lil Mo pointed to the river.

"So they're making camp?"

"Looks like it," said Lil Mo.

"That's not a bad thing," Funi Man said. "They are not afraid of being seen. That means they are not planning an attack. Not yet. They are respecting us. They know we have good fighters in our town."

"What will happen now?" asked Lil Mo.

"We wait. After the Choctaw council meets, we do what they say."

Lil Mo and Funi Man watched the men till the torch burned out.

"Why don't you and I both keep an eye out, just to be safe?" said Funi Man.

"I'd like that fine," said Lil Mo.

Funi Man and Lil Mo spent the first hour in silence. They watched for any movement on the river, in the woods, or from the campsite.

"Lil Mo," Funi Man finally said, "you grew up close to us. But we Choctaws see the world very differently from people across Bok Chitto."

"I already like it better here," said Lil Mo.

"Good," said Funi Man. "Would you like to learn about Choctaws?"

"Yes."

"Hoke. Choctaw children grow up hearing stories and being taught things," said Funi Man. "What I'm gonna tell you tonight might take a Choctaw child several years to learn. But you're older. You are smart and listen well. And we don't have several years."

"Yakoke," said Lil Mo. Funi Man smiled.

"First, Lil Mo, you have to trust Koi Losa. Do what he does, do everything he says to do. Ask him why later, but when you are in the woods or near the river, do what he says. He is the best watcher in Choctaw town, even though he's only a boy."

"I will," said Lil Mo. "He climbs a tree like a squirrel. He is fast!"

"Yes, he is," said Funi Man. "Do you remember what *Koi Losa* means?"

"'Black Panther,'" said Lil Mo.

"Good, yes," Funi Man said, smiling and nodding. "Koi Losa means 'Black Panther.' To Choctaws, the panther is just about the most sacred of all animals. Panthers are your kinfolk from long ago, your ancestors. If you see a panther, it is both a warning and a blessing.

"The warning is that your life is in danger. You should watch every step you take. You should think about what you are planning, about who your friends are. Are they honest and truthful?"

"Why is a panther a blessing?" asked Lil Mo.

"The panther might be someone you didn't even know. But you have respected the memory of your family. The ancestors like that. When they see you are in danger, they warn you. The panther is there to protect you from the danger."

"I understand why Koi Losa has that name. He protects good people from danger."

"That's right, Lil Mo," said Funi Man. "You are a smart young man. Do you know the Choctaw word for 'good people'?"

"No."

"Okla chukma. That means 'good people' in Choctaw."

"Okla chukma," said Lil Mo.

Funi Man smiled and nodded. "You'll be speaking Choctaw before the year is out," he said.

"Why is Koi Losa called Black Panther, instead of just Panther?" asked Lil Mo.

"A black panther is the most powerful of all panthers," said Funi Man.

Lil Mo nodded. "I'm lucky to call him my friend," he said.

"Yes, you are," said Funi Man. He took a long breath and looked to the treetops. "Now, I should tell you about owls."

The leaves rustled, and Funi Man waited. He almost expected to hear swooping wings, to see outstretched owl claws flying at them. Nothing happened. The stars twinkled bright, and Funi Man knew that he and Lil Mo were in no danger, at least not tonight.

"The safest thing to do is avoid owls, all owls," he said. "Some are messengers. But they always bring bad news. They tell you when someone close to you has died."

"Do they talk?" asked Lil Mo.

"Well, not exactly," said Funi Man. "They might land in a tree near your door. They might fly overhead when you walk through the woods. They howl and hoot till you know they are calling to you."

"That sounds scary," said Lil Mo.

"It is scary," said Funi Man. "But these are the friendly owls. Some owls are much worse. Some are witches, bad witches. They live deep in the woods and change themselves from people into owls. They fly at night and cause trouble. Whenever you hear the call of an owl, leave if you can. Go another way. If you can't go, be very careful. If you hear an owl call, trust no one you see. Unless you know them very well, trust no one."

"Why don't Choctaws kill the owls?" asked Lil Mo. "If they're so bad?"

"Sometimes we do," said Funi Man. "But you don't always know if a person is an owl—a bad witch—or an alikchi."

"A what?"

"An alikchi," said Funi Man. "An alikchi is a good medicine person. An alikchi can heal a sickness. And an alikchi can protect you from bad things happening."

"Do you know any alikchis?" asked Lil Mo.

"Oh, yes," said Funi Man, laughing. "I know a very powerful alikchi. Her name is Shonti."

"Is she funny, too?" asked Lil Mo.

"No, Lil Mo," said Funi Man. "She is not funny, but she is strange. You see, she has some very unusual friends. Six big rattlesnakes. They go with her everywhere. You can't always see them, but trust me, they are there."

"I hate rattlesnakes!" said Lil Mo. "They're dangerous!"

"Most everybody does," said Funi Man. "But not Choctaws. You have seen the diamonds we sew on our clothes? For special times, like the Miracle Night when your family crossed the river. The women had diamonds on their sleeves. Did you notice?"

"Yes," said Lil Mo. "I remember."

"The diamonds honor the rattlesnake, the diamonds on his back. We respect the rattlesnake. Lil Mo, you must never kill a rattlesnake. Give him his space. Walk away slowly if you hear his rattle, but never hurt a rattlesnake. They are protectors also."

Lil Mo looked to the dark woods surrounding them. He stared at the tree limbs overhead. He narrowed his eyes at patches of leaves on the ground, looking for rattlesnakes. Everything in the woods seemed more alive than before. He understood why Koi Losa listened and watched everything as if his life depended on it.

His life does depend on it, thought Lil Mo. *And so does mine.*

Funi Man put his arm over Lil Mo's shoulder, and the two sat watching the moonlight ripple on the river.

"So," said Lil Mo, "I know about owls and panthers and rattlesnakes."

"You know enough to get you by for a while," said Funi Man. "Let's say lesson number one is over. You think about what you've learned, and let's keep our eyes sharp."

"Hoke," said Lil Mo.

Soon the fog thickened, and the moon and stars disappeared. The woods were silent. No frogs, no owls, no creeping panthers or rattling snakes broke the silence, only the sleeping sounds of Lil Mo's closest kin. Both Lil Mo and Funi Man stayed awake till morning, feeling safe in the company of family.

CHAPTER 17

Secret Cave of Friendship

After a breakfast of bread and corn pashofa, Lil Mo took a quiet stroll through the woods while Koi Losa watched from the trees overhead.

I don't want to wait for the next full moon to see Joseph, he thought. *I want to see him today.*

He looked to the treetops to see if Koi Losa was watching him. Then he smiled at himself. "He could be four feet from me and I wouldn't know it," he whispered. "Nobody can hide like Koi Losa! I'll just have to take my chances."

He ducked under a clump of bushes and crawled to the last place he had seen Joseph, the crossing place. Lil Mo scooted on his belly under the bushes, close enough to watch the other side of the river without being seen. The ground was wet and muddy, and he curled into a ball, wrapping his arms around his knees.

"What am I doing here, anyway?" he asked himself. "My family is safe—for now. But if the plantation guards see me, they'll cross the river and come after us all. But I miss Joseph. Will I ever see him again?"

He didn't have to wait long for the answer.

Joseph stepped from the shadow of an oak tree and tossed a stone across the river. It landed with a loud *PLOP* a few feet from Lil Mo, splashing water on his face.

"Whooo!" said Lil Mo, then covered his mouth and hoped no one had heard him. He stood up and waved at Joseph.

Joseph waved back, then motioned for Lil Mo to cross the river. Lil Mo nodded, and Joseph turned away and took off in a mad dash. He knew Lil Mo would know where to meet him—their secret cave above the cotton fields, where they had been meeting for years.

Lil Mo considered crossing on the stones. *If they're watching the river closely, they will be watching there,* he thought. He hurried downstream to a shady spot, where cottonwood trees hung their limbs over the river. He waded into the water, watching for any sign of men on the plantation side.

When he was certain no one saw him, he gulped a big breath of air and dove underwater. Kicking his legs and pushing with his lean, strong arms, Lil Mo swam across the Bok Chitto River. Underwater.

His head soon popped up above the chilly river waters. Lil Mo studied the shore. He saw no one. He crawled from the river, staying close to the ground. He took off his shirt and twisted it tight, wringing out the water.

"Brrrr," he said. He ran his hands across his pants and stomped his feet. Water dripped and splashed. Still wet and cold, Lil Mo crossed the cotton field, staying close to the ground. The other slaves, the people his family had had to leave behind, were picking cotton in another field. Lil Mo knew that the guards would be watching up and down the river. He dropped to the ground to listen several times, but heard nothing.

Soon Joseph stood and welcomed Lil Mo to their hideout.

"You're wet!" he said.

"Yep," said Lil Mo. "I just dove in and swam."

"Thank you," said Joseph. "You are a real friend."

"You, too, Joseph. You know about the campsite on this side of the river? The guards are close, but at least they're not trying to cross the river and capture us. What have you heard?"

"Nothing much. I've talked to my father, but he doesn't know anything."

Lil Mo took off his shoes and socks and laid his pants on the boulder to dry. "I've got to find another way to cross the river," he said. "I'm freezing!"

For the first time that day, Joseph laughed.

"Don't laugh at me! I'm cold. And I'm your best friend in the world."

"You are my best friend," said Joseph. "And I wish you didn't live across the river."

"Me, too. But I am glad, too, 'cause I have a chance there. My family is free. Free from Bledsoe's whip."

"Yeah," said Joseph. "Bledsoe's whip. I'm afraid for my father."

"Why?'

"Bledsoe put him in the slave jail. He is so mad, I'm afraid he'll take his whip to my father."

"What can we do?" asked Lil Mo.

"Let's think," said Joseph. "We can come up with something."

The boys retreated to two hideaways they'd built years ago, when their friendship was young and they played with the innocence of children who would never get caught. Lil Mo climbed beneath a fat boulder to a cave he had dug in the soft black earth.

Joseph climbed to his treehouse and let his eyes wander across the field. He scanned the plantation grounds, from the river to the big white plantation house. He watched for anyone coming their way.

Smoke still rose from the camp by the river. Field workers stooped and stood, picking cotton bolls and tossing them in sacks slung over their shoulders. Guards held their shotguns and walked slowly up and down the cotton rows.

"We're safe here for a while," Joseph said. He had no way of knowing he was about to enter a Choctaw world, Shonti's world—of rattlesnakes and danger.

CHAPTER 18

Shonti and the Rattlesnakes

Lil Mo entered the small cave and crawled to his sitting spot, with his back against the wall. He brushed dirt from his arms and legs. *I hope nobody comes and sees my clothes on the boulder*, he thought. *Nope, Joseph will keep a good watch out.*

Lil Mo turned his thoughts to the problem.

"How can we stop Bledsoe from hurting Mr. Porter?" he whispered. As soon as the words left his lips, he felt the air of the cave grow warm. His skin felt hot, and sweat dripped from his eyebrows, blinding him. He blinked and rubbed his eyes.

When his sight cleared, he saw the smoky figure of an old Choctaw woman sitting in the cave. A bundle of gray hair circled her round, friendly face. The old woman smiled. Lil Mo could see the wall behind her—through her—as she sat in front of him.

"Who are you?' he asked.

"I am Shonti," the woman said. "I live in Choctaw town. I'm here to help you."

"Why?" asked Lil Mo.

"Because you are okla chukma, good people, and that's what I do. I am alikchi. Some people would call me a medicine woman. I help okla chukma when they are in trouble."

"Can you help Joseph's father?" asked Lil Mo.

"Oh, yes, I think I can," said Shonti. "He is okla chukma, too, you know."

"Yes, and so is Joseph."

"Yes, and he is your best friend."

"You know about us? About our friendship?"

"Yes," said Shonti. "How do you think I knew about this hiding place? I know secrets on both sides of the river."

"How?" asked Lil Mo.

"I have friends that tell me things," said Shonti. Her mouth quivered in an almost smile. "Do you want to meet them?"

"I'm not so sure," said Lil Mo. "I think Funi Man told me about your friends. You sure it's safe?"

Shonti lifted her chin in laughter. "Yes, Lil Mo. Nobody gets hurt. Not here, anyway," she said. "Now remember, there is nothing to be afraid of."

The cave grew darker than ever. Shonti vanished, or at least her body did. Her smiling, friendly face floated before him in the darkness. Lil Mo drew his knees to his chest and froze.

"Don't move," said Shonti. She looked at the ground. Lil Mo heard the soft rattle on the floor of the cave.

Rattlesnake! he thought. *This is what Funi Man was telling me. I am not ready for this!*

If Lil Mo was not ready for one rattlesnake, he would never be ready for what happened next. A whirring sound rose from the ground behind him. Lil Mo felt something wriggle across the skin of his bare back.

"Yooow!" he yelled, then quickly covered his mouth.

"Not good," said Shonti. "You never want to startle a rattlesnake."

"Sorry," Lil Mo whispered. His eyes grew large, and his mouth clamped shut. The rattlesnake wrapped around his waist, tightening itself like a thick rope. He shivered to feel the slick underbelly and scratchy scales as the snake slid over his knees and curled at his feet.

"There are more," said Shonti. As if in reply, five snakes surrounded Lil Mo and began their rattlesnake songs.

"You should feel better now," said Shonti. "You have lots of friends."

"Yes," said Lil Mo. "I feel so much better, sitting in a cave surrounded by rattlesnakes. I am one lucky little boy."

"You are just like Funi Man said," Shonti replied with a smile.

"But how will the snakes help Joseph's father?" he asked.

"Lil Mo, my rattlesnakes know about okla chukma and will protect them. They are Choctaw rattlesnakes." The rattlesnakes whirred louder. "I would not want to be Mr. Bledsoe today," said Shonti.

"Lil Mo!" Joseph's head appeared at the cave opening.

Shonti lifted her eyebrows and looked at Lil Mo.

"You decide," she whispered.

"I want him to know everything," Lil Mo said.

"Good," said Shonti. "Joseph, come in. Make yourself comfortable, and be careful not to step on any rattlesnakes."

Joseph looked ready to run.

"It's all right, Joseph," said Lil Mo. "Come in. This is Shonti, a Choctaw friend. She's here to help us."

"Is it safe?" asked Joseph. Lil Mo nodded and patted the ground beside him, and Joseph took his seat.

"I brought some rattlesnake friends with me," said Shonti. "One of them is already on his way to take care of Bledsoe."

She lifted and lowered her arm like a slow wave washing on the beach, then pointed to the wall behind her. A cloud of soft light appeared, and inside the light was Joseph's father. He sat on the sawdust floor and leaned against the wall of the jail. His head was buried in his knees.

"Is he hurt?" asked Joseph.

Shonti wrapped her arm around his shoulder and pulled him close, saying, "No, Joseph. Your father is not hurt, and he will not *be* hurt."

The scene on the cave wall changed. Bledsoe appeared, snapping his whip and driving his wagon. He gritted his teeth in a mean snarl, then jerked the reins and brought the wagon to a sudden stop beside the barn.

"No!" yelled Joseph. "He's going to whip my father."

"Just watch," Shonti whispered. "My friend will protect him."

Bledsoe grabbed his whip from the wagon, spit on the ground, and pushed the barn door open. He walked from stall to stall in the barn, dragging the leather strap of his whip. He paused at the door to the jail. Eyeing the whip, Mr. Porter rose to his feet and backed against the wall.

"We missed you in the fields today," said Bledsoe. With a wicked twist of his mouth, he made up a story of the morning—a bold and bitter lie—to watch the pain it caused.

"Your son Zeke fired his shotgun at that slave boy across the river. The boy was playing right out in the open, not worried about a thing. You should have been there."

Mr. Porter flinched.

"You're wondering if that little dark boy is still alive? You will know soon enough," said Bledsoe. "Right now we have other business to attend to."

He flung open the door.

"Turn around." He pushed Mr. Porter against the wall, grabbing his collar and tearing his shirt open. "Put your hands against the wall!"

"I have always been loyal to you," said Mr. Porter. "You don't know what we saw that night."

"I don't care what you saw," said Bledsoe. He spoke softly, hissing his words. "I only know what you did. You let five slaves escape. Now you will suffer for what you did. Suffer for the rest of your life. The scars from my whip never heal, Sam Porter. And I never forget."

Mr. Porter heard the soft whirring sound before Bledsoe did. His quick glance fell to the sawdust floor. He expected to see a rattlesnake curled up and ready to strike. Instead, he saw the other end of Bledsoe's whip, writhing on the floor. The leather quivered and began to change, first at the tip.

Inch by inch Mr. Porter saw the change. The dark leather rope of the whip softened in color, till the diamond pattern of a rattlesnake emerged. The whip grew shorter and thickened. Everything happened quickly. Bledsoe knew nothing. He saw only the man in front of him, Sam Porter, ready to take a beating for his beliefs.

Bledsoe no longer held a twelve-foot-long whip with a wooden handle. Instead, he held a seven-foot-long rattlesnake. He whipped the snake over Mr. Porter's shoulder.

Bledsoe jerked in surprise. The snake was strong and knew where it wanted to go. It curled itself around Mr. Porter's neck. Its mouth opened wide and it whipped itself to a stop, two inches from Porter's face.

Mr. Porter held his breath, staring at the fang-filled mouth before him. The snake slowly closed its mouth and dipped its head in an eerie show of respect for Mr. Porter. With a quiet slithering of muscle, the snake unfurled from the prisoner and leapt at Bledsoe.

Bledsoe reached for his pistol, but the snake was lightning fast. It struck Bledsoe on the palm and sank its fangs deep, whipping its thick body through the air. Bledsoe fired his pistol, and a shower of splinters fell from the ceiling.

The scene on the cave wall clouded. Lil Mo and Joseph shook their heads and rubbed their eyes to see.

"What happened?" asked Joseph. "What will Bledsoe do to my father?"

"You have seen enough for today," said Shonti. "I can only tell you that Mr. Bledsoe will be carrying his whip in his left hand for at least a month. He will be more afraid of your father than your father ever was of him. And

Bledsoe is right about one thing. Some scars never heal. My rattlesnake friend left Bledsoe with a scar to make him think twice before he shakes a whip at your father again, Joseph."

"Thank you," said Joseph. "My father is a good man."

"Yes, I know. Okla chukma. That's what we Choctaws say. Sam Porter is okla chukma."

Shonti watched as Lil Mo and Joseph parted with a tight hug and handshake. *They are so innocent*, she thought. *Evil is so close, and these two are so innocent and happy.*

CHAPTER 19

A Pup for Lil Mo

One week later

From where he slept, Lil Mo looked through the door of the lean-to, staring at the dark canyons on the bright yellow moon. On the plantation side of the river, Joseph stared through the open window of his room at the same full moon. That night, the first full moon after Miracle Night, Reddog gave birth to four fine puppies.

When he saw a lantern light outside, Joseph leapt out of bed, threw his clothes on, and hurried to Reddog's sleeping spot in the barn. His mother was already there.

"Look," she said. "Four healthy puppies. Reddog did well tonight."

"Which was born first?" asked Joseph.

His mother pointed to a yellow-and-red male puppy. His eyes were closed, and he pawed at Reddog's belly. Joseph thought, *This puppy is Lil Mo's. I've got to get it to him!*

He picked up the pup and felt his tiny wet ears. The pup licked his hands. Joseph beamed. "I love this little pup," he said.

"He's a beauty," his mother replied. "Now, you can stay for a while, but only a little while. Just be careful and don't hold him too long. Reddog will get nervous, and she's had a long night already."

"I'll be quiet and careful," said Joseph. "Thanks for letting me stay."

Joseph held the new pup till Reddog lifted her eyes to him. He placed the pup at her belly and watched Reddog care for the puppies, licking and nuzzling from one pup to the next. "Lil Mo will love his puppy," he whispered.

After breakfast that morning, he asked his mother, "When I finish my chores, can I tell my friends about the puppies? I'll be back this afternoon."

"That'll be fine," Mrs. Porter said.

Joseph broke his own speed record for morning chores: feeding chickens and hogs and cleaning yesterday's tools in less than an hour.

"I'm gone!" he hollered through the back door. Joseph walked at a normal speed, but once out of sight of the kitchen window, he broke into a run. He crossed the fields and hurried to the river, staying low to the ground as he ran. He stopped often, looking over his shoulder, making sure Harold didn't see him.

"He'll be here!" Joseph said out loud. "He remembers the full moon. He's gonna be here!"

He knelt as he neared the river. The ground was wet and his knees sank in the mud. He crawled through a thicket of plants, breathing hard, and sat down on a small log on the water's edge. Anyone from the Choctaw side of Bok Chitto could see him. His eyes scanned the far bank.

Only a few minutes passed before Lil Mo stepped from behind a cypress tree on the other side. Joseph wanted to shout and wave, but he knew better. He tossed a stone in the water to catch Lil Mo's attention.

When Lil Mo saw him, a grin spread across his face. He clenched his fists and jumped. When he landed, he slipped in the mud and rolled into the river. Joseph laughed as Lil Mo ducked his head and swam to join him. He pulled Lil Mo from the river, and they stood in the bushes, smiling and staring at each other.

"I was hoping you would remember we always meet at full moon," Joseph said.

"I could never forget that, Joseph."

"I have good news for you," Joseph said. "Reddog gave birth to her puppies, and the firstborn pup is yours!"

"I can have my own pup?" asked Lil Mo. "That is great news!"

"Will the Choctaws let you have a pup?"

"Oh, yes," said Lil Mo. "The Choctaws love dogs. Every family has a dog and treats it like a favorite child."

Joseph smiled. "Times are hard," he said, "but we can still be happy."

"Hoke, so when can I get this pup?"

"Tonight," said Joseph. "Meet me here at the river at midnight."

"See you then," Lil Mo said, glancing at the tree where Koi Losa hid and watched them talk. "Chi pisa la chike," he said over his shoulder as he dove into the river and returned to his Choctaw home.

In his excitement, Joseph forgot to crouch as he ran home. He swatted at the grass and covered the ground in leaps.

"Mother!" he shouted, bounding through the back door. "Everyone is really happy about the new pups!"

"No one could be as happy as you are," his mother replied.

Joseph was more helpful than ever that day. He carried water for the washing and even scrubbed the shirts on the washboard. He carried the laundry to the clothesline, saying, "You work too hard sometimes, Mother. Let me hang the clothes for you."

Joseph helped with the cooking, carried lunch to the field for his brother, and ran home looking for something else to do.

"Son, you're making me tired just watching you," Mrs. Porter said, shaking her head

The day moved at a slow crawl. The faster Joseph worked, the slower the sun rolled across the sky.

During supper, Joseph realized he still had a problem. *A big problem,* he thought. *Mother will notice—and so will Zeke—that one of the pups is missing. I can't lie to her!*

Then just as quickly, he realized he'd better be careful. *She's not a regular mother. She's a mind reader.*

"Mother, this is the best corn bread you have ever made!" he said, grabbing another piece.

"Thank you, Joseph," his mother said, tilting her head in that way she had of asking, *What is going on with you?*

Joseph said nothing. He stuffed the corn bread into his mouth and wiped dripping butter from his lips.

After supper, he cleared the table and dumped the leftovers in the scrap bucket. Without thinking, he tossed them out the back door for the dogs.

"Be sure to save some for Reddog," his mother reminded him. Joseph raced to the scraps and scrambled with the dogs. He even outwrestled Jumper, the biggest dog, for a pork bone.

"You'll get extra tomorrow, I promise," he said,

dashing to the barn to feed Reddog. As he stepped through the door, he heard someone behind him. Expecting to see Zeke, he turned and said, "I bet Reddog's hungry," but his words stuck in his throat.

Harold stood blocking the door, with a shotgun balanced on his hip. "You sure are happy today," he said. "Running home from the river. What were you doing there anyway?"

"Nothing," Joseph said.

"Nothing? You were running from the spot where the slaves crossed the river. You trying to tell me you were doing nothing?"

"I was fishing."

"Funny way of fishing, without a pole. And no bait, neither. You're lying to me," Harold said.

Joseph was not afraid of Harold, even though Harold was older and bigger, but he was afraid of what Harold might tell Bledsoe. "I wasn't doing anything. I don't know where they crossed the river. I was playing, that's all."

"Why did you lie to me?"

"Because you aren't my mother or my father," Joseph said. He stood as tall as he could and stared at Harold. "I don't have to tell you anything!"

Harold stepped back in surprise. "You better watch yourself," he said. "I have my eye on you." He slung his shotgun over his shoulder and slapped his fist against the wall as he left the shed.

Joseph was angry with himself for not being more careful running back from the river. He took a deep breath and knelt by Reddog.

"You doing all right, lady? You know I'll take good care of you. You did real good last night. Four puppies, and every one of them strong and healthy."

He leaned close to Reddog and lifted her ear. He glanced over his shoulder, making sure Harold was gone. "Lil Mo gets one of your pups tonight," he whispered. "I know you're gonna miss him. I will, too. But you can see him sometime. I don't know when, but somehow you can see him again. I promise."

CHAPTER 20

Late-Night River Crossing

"How was Reddog?" asked Mrs. Porter as Joseph entered the kitchen.

"She looks tired, but she's doing fine." Joseph said nothing about Harold. He helped with the dishes, but without the joy in his step.

"What's wrong, Joseph?" his mother asked. "I think it's about time you told me what's happening. I know you're excited about the pups, but something else is going on. Is this about your father? Do you know something you're not telling me?"

"No, it's not about Dad."

"Joseph?"

"I'm sorry, Mother. Please don't get mad at me. Dad knows. It was his idea." Mrs. Porter sat down at the mention of her husband, and lines of worry swept across her face. "Mother, you can't tell anyone. Not Zeke or anyone. If Bledsoe finds out, it'll be bad."

"I'll be careful. Your father is in jail. Of course I won't tell anyone. But first you need to tell me. Come here, son."

Joseph reached out his arms and held his mother. For the first time in his life, Joseph felt like a grown-up in his mother's arms. She held him tight, but she was not soothing and comforting him, as a mother would a child. Joseph was comforting his mother.

"I am bringing one of the pups to a friend," he said.

"Well, you need to wait till he's older and ready to leave Reddog. It's not safe for a pup to leave his mother so soon after birth. You know that, son."

"It has to be now. Before anyone gets to know the pup."

"Joseph, what is the secret you're not telling me?"

Joseph took a long breath before he spoke. "I am bringing the pup to my friend across the river. Dad said you know about him. Lil Mo. Please don't be mad."

"When?"

"Tonight. Lil Mo swam across the river, and we talked."

"Did anyone see you?"

"No," Joseph said.

"Oh, Joseph," his mother said, wiping tears from her

eyes. "Do you know the risk you're taking?"

"Yes. I'm careful. Mother, can I tell you something else?"

"Please. Yes, tell me."

"Lil Mo is still my best friend."

"I remember the day you met Lil Mo," she said. "You were not even two years old, and you wandered off in the woods. You were playing with Lil Mo when your father found you, just sitting on the ground playing the peep-eye game."

"Mother."

"Yes?"

"Dad is a good man, isn't he?'

"Yes, son. Your father is a good man. And he is proud of you. You must be very careful and not do anything that could hurt your father."

"I promise I won't. No one knows about tonight. Just you and me and Pa."

"Joseph, you should know the risk, taking a pup away from her mother the day after he's born."

"What can I do?"

"Well, maybe I can milk Reddog. She won't milk like a cow, but I can get some milk. I'll catch it in a jar with a cork, and you can bring it tonight. And be sure to tell Lil Mo to find another mother dog to take care of him."

"There are plenty of dogs in Choctaw town," said

Joseph. "I hear them barking all day long—hunting dogs, watchdogs. Lil Mo says they love dogs."

His mother stood and wiped her face with her apron. "Your brother should be here soon. He's taking supper to your father tonight," she said. "As soon as he leaves, I'll put the milk jar in a leather pouch and hide it in a corner of the barn, near Reddog. You can carry the pup in the pouch, too."

Joseph nodded.

"And Joseph? Be sure to tell your father how much I miss him. When you see him tonight, will you tell him that?"

"I promise, Mother. He misses you, too, you know."

In a short while Zeke appeared at the back door. He left carrying a plate of pork chops and potatoes for his father. Half an hour later, Joseph jumped out of bed, already dressed. He sped to the water bucket and scooped a cup for his father.

Walking fast and trying his best not to stumble, Joseph was more nervous than ever. He missed Reddog running at his side. He was both excited and terrified about delivering the pup to Lil Mo.

What if Harold suspects something and tells Bledsoe? What if the pup dies? What if Lil Mo gets caught?

As soon as he saw his father, his fears vanished. His father greeted him with his first true smile in a month.

"So tell me, son, did you see Lil Mo? Is tonight the night?"

"Yes, Dad. I'm bringing Lil Mo the pup tonight, and Mother knows all about it. But don't worry. She's a better secret keeper than I am. She knows not to tell anybody."

"Well, I would be lying if I told you I wasn't worried, son. But I know you will be careful. You know, this is a special night for Lil Mo—and for you. Are you excited?"

"I can't wait," said Joseph. "But I am afraid, too."

"You are not crossing the river, are you?"

"No, he's coming over here."

"You know he is risking his life, son?"

Joseph nodded. "Lil Mo is meeting me around the bend, downstream from the crossing place. We think it's safer there."

"Just make certain no one is following you," said Mr. Porter. "Son, be very, very careful. If anything happens to you, I will never forgive myself."

"I feel the same way about you, Dad. Mother says she misses you. We all do."

"I know, son. I'm thinking maybe in a few days I'll be out of here."

Joseph reached through the bars and gripped his father's hands. "Good night, Dad. I'll have good news for you tomorrow. I promise."

"I can use good news, son. Good luck!"

Joseph hurried home, trying not to make a sound. The

light was out in the house. He entered the tool shed, stepping quietly.

Reddog whimpered a welcome at Joseph, lifting her head to see him. The pups lay asleep across her belly. Joseph found the leather pouch and knelt by the pups.

He patted Reddog on the hindquarters and slipped the pup into the pouch. Reddog watched him with a careful eye. As he moved to the shadows, she rolled over and began nursing the three remaining pups.

"Good dog," Joseph whispered. He wrapped both arms around the pouch, held it close to his chest, and slipped from the barn.

The moon ducked behind the clouds for only a moment, and Joseph dashed to the rear of the house. Seeing no sign of Harold, he sped to the river, crouching as he ran. When he reached the shore, he knelt with his back against a pine tree. With soft and careful fingers, he felt inside the pouch for the pup.

"You'll be home soon," he whispered, rubbing the soft belly of the new pup.

He did not have long to wait. Joseph expected Lil Mo to float across the river, clinging to a log. He never expected what he saw—a boat!

Lil Mo was paddling a boat across the Bok Chitto River!

The boat was long and slender, and Lil Mo was hunched over, with a blanket covering his head and shoulders. He clutched a thick paddle and dipped it from side to side into the water. Joseph stood frozen as the boat slipped across the river without a sound and eased onto the muddy bank.

Joseph stepped from the shadows and pulled the boat ashore. "A beautiful boat," he whispered. "Great job."

Lil Mo said nothing.

"No one's here. It's all right, Lil Mo," said Joseph, yanking the blanket from his friend's shoulders. The blanket fell to the ground. Joseph stepped back. A shiver of fear ran down his spine. The young man standing before him was not Lil Mo.

"Who are you?" Joseph stammered. "Where's Lil Mo?"

CHAPTER 21

Joseph Meets Martha Tom

The boy pointed across the river where Lil Mo waited. Several Choctaw men surrounded Lil Mo to protect him, all holding shotguns aimed and ready to fire.

"I'm his friend, Koi Losa," said the boy. "Funi Man thought it safer if I took the pup."

"I was hoping to see Lil Mo. I don't know Funi Man, but he's right. This is safer." Joseph tried to hide his disappointment. "Here's the pup. He's the best of the litter. There's a jar, too, with milk from his mother. Will there be a mother dog in Choctaw town to raise him?" he asked.

"Yes, we found a good mother for him today," said Koi Losa. "Her pups are a week old."

He took the pup without looking inside the bag and placed it in the boat. Joseph saw another blanket covering the floor of the boat. When Koi Losa stepped to the boat, the blanket moved.

"I want to see the puppy!" said a muffled voice. Koi Losa flipped the blanket aside. There sat Martha Tom!

"Halito," she said, and stood to greet him. Joseph's jaw dropped and his ears turned pink-red.

Martha Tom rocked back and forth in the boat, bit her bottom lip, and finally covered her mouth to keep from laughing.

"Hey!" Koi Losa said. "Stop rocking! You're gonna tip the boat over!"

"Sorry," said Martha Tom, stepping onto the shore. "You are Joseph?" she said, turning her attention to the speechless boy before her. "Lil Mo talks about you all the time. I'm very happy to meet you."

Joseph had imagined what his first meeting with Martha Tom would be like. From the first time he saw her, the Miracle Night, he always pictured her as magical, not a real person who might stub her toe or feel the sting of a mosquito.

Not Martha Tom! She floated, she sang, she walked across rivers. She led good people to freedom, that's what Martha Tom did! Now here she was, and he couldn't think of a word to say.

"Yes, I'm Joseph. And, yes, Lil Mo is my best friend. So where is he?" He saw Lil Mo waiting across the river along the bank. "Oh, yeah, I see him," he stammered, and quickly waved at Lil Mo. Then his eyes locked on Martha Tom's feet. "Yeah, there he is. I saw him, right over there. See him? 'Hello, Lil Mo.' I think he sees me. So you are Martha Tom, and I think I told you my name is Joseph."

He stopped to catch his breath.

"Hoke," said Martha Tom, trying to keep from laughing. "This is good, our meeting. Now we should be going."

She sat down, and Koi Losa pushed the boat from the shore.

"I almost forgot," Martha Tom said. "Lil Mo wanted you to know he is naming the pup after you. He says he'll think about you every time he calls his pup."

Joseph felt his clumsiness slip away.

"Tell him I said—how did you say it? Thank you?"

"Yakoke," said Koi Losa.

"Yakoke," Joseph repeated. "Tell Lil Mo his friend Joseph says yakoke."

As Joseph stood on the riverbank, watching the boat disappear into the fog, he could not stop thinking about his conversation with Martha Tom. "That was so dumb! How could I be so dumb! What will she tell Lil Mo?" He wanted to jump in the river and swim across, just to let Martha Tom know he wasn't an idiot.

"No, I think maybe that would convince her I *am* an

idiot," he muttered. As he turned to leave, Joseph picked up a pinecone and hurled it against a tree trunk. The cone shattered and popped.

Hearing the sound, Joseph suddenly remembered where he was. The evening was not about Martha Tom and how she felt about him. This was a very dangerous night, a very special night, a night of giving Lil Mo his pup.

"His first gift from my family," he whispered to himself. Joseph looked to the sky, and the moon shone brighter than ever.

<hr />

On the Choctaw side, Martha Tom stepped from the boat with the puppy in her arms. "He's beautiful," she said, handing the puppy to Lil Mo.

"Did you tell him?" Lil Mo asked. "Does he know I'm naming the pup after him?"

"Yes, I promised you I'd tell him."

"What did he say?"

"He said to tell you yakoke," Martha Tom said with a smile.

"Joseph said yakoke? All right!" He looked to the far side, but Joseph was gone. The pup wriggled in his arms and whined. Lil Mo held him tight to his chest.

"He's warm," he said. "You doing hoke, boy? You're home now. Home with me and the Choctaws. You're gonna like it here."

"You have a fine-looking dog," said Funi Man, stepping from behind a tree. "Can I hold him?" Lil Mo handed his new puppy to Funi Man. With the threat of trouble gone, several other Choctaw men made their way quietly to their own homes.

"We need to get him to his new mother," said Funi Man. "So what will you call him?"

"*Ofi*. That's the word for *dog* in Choctaw, right?" Lil Mo asked.

"That's right. You're learning, son."

Lil Mo beamed. "Ofijo. That's what we'll call him," he said. "Jo-dog, for Joseph. What do you think?"

"I like it hoke," said Funi Man.

"I like it, too," said Martha Tom. "Can I hold him?"

Lil Mo, Martha Tom, and Funi Man traded Ofijo back and forth as they walked from the riverbank to the lean-to.

"You can keep him for tonight only," said Funi Man. "Feed him milk when he whines. Pour just a little on a rag and let him suck it."

"Where is the mother dog?" asked Lil Mo.

"I'll take care of that tomorrow morning," said Funi Man. "You don't need to be wandering around town.

We can visit Ofijo every day till he's old enough to live with you."

"I can't wait," Lil Mo said. "I've never had a pup before."

"You'll be a step closer to being true Choctaw," said Funi Man. "Every Choctaw needs a dog."

"Are there any stories about Choctaw dogs?" Lil Mo asked.

"Yes," said Funi Man. "There's a real scary story about a man, his dog, and a Choctaw ghost. But no stories tonight."

Lil Mo said good-bye to Funi Man and Martha Tom and stooped to enter the lean-to. He laid Ofijo in his sleeping corner and was about to crawl under his blanket when he heard scratching on the outside wall. He peered through the cracks and saw Koi Losa.

"Just a minute," he whispered, and moved to join Koi Losa.

"I'm happy for you, Lil Mo," said Koi Losa.

"Yakoke," Lil Mo said. "I was wondering where you went."

"I have been watching the river," Koi Losa said. "I had to be sure no one saw the boat. That was Funi Man's idea."

"He's a smart man," Lil Mo said. "He thinks of everything."

"He cares for you," Koi Losa replied. "Do you

understand about a Choctaw uncle?"

"I know what an uncle is," said Lil Mo. "How is a Choctaw uncle different?"

"A Choctaw uncle can be your kin, but he doesn't have to be. Funi Man is your uncle. He will teach you everything he knows. He'll be like a second father to you."

"I had a couple of aunties on the plantation who looked after me when my mother was busy with work," Lil Mo said quietly. "I like that, having Funi Man as my uncle."

"Good," said Koi Losa. "There are plans for a ceremony. But I have probably said too much. I'll stay and keep watch."

"Yakoke, Koi Losa," said Lil Mo. "This is my best day so far in Choctaw town. Good night." He settled into his corner of the lean-to, and soon he and Ofijo were sound asleep.

CHAPTER 22

Harold Follows Joseph

As excited as he was about Lil Mo and his new puppy, Joseph knew he was taking too many chances. *They'll be watching me closer than ever*, he thought. *If they catch me with Lil Mo, Dad will pay the price. He doesn't deserve to be punished, to be sleeping in a barn with a chain around his leg. Dad needs to be home.*

The next night, with the help of his mother, Joseph put a bold plan into action—a plan to bring his father home.

One A.M.

Joseph crept around the corner of his house, crouching

in the shadows. He hid in a clump of bushes, careful and quiet. When he spotted Harold dozing against a tree by the barn, he slipped a handful of pinecones from his pocket.

He can't wait to use that shotgun, Joseph thought, *and tonight it will work against him*. He took a deep breath and tossed the pinecones at the door to the barn.

"What was that?" Harold said, jerking awake. "I heard something!"

The puppies woke up, and barks and yelps filled the night air. Harold dashed around the barn and flung the door open.

"I've got you now!" he hollered, stepping through the door and shouldering his shotgun.

A light came on in the kitchen.

"What is it?" Mrs. Porter stuck her head through the door, holding a lantern.

"Ma'am," said Harold, "I heard someone in your barn and I know it was Joseph, on his way to help Mr. Porter escape!"

"You saw Joseph? That can't be. He is in his bed and sound asleep."

"Ma'am," said Harold, "I am a guard, appointed by Mr. Bledsoe himself, to watch out for anyone leaving your house at night."

"Oh," said Mrs. Porter. "Well, let me know if there's

any trouble." She stepped inside and placed the lantern on the kitchen table.

Harold stood in the yard, looking from the barn to the porch, not knowing what to do. "Mrs. Porter," he shouted, "may I borrow your lantern?"

"Of course," she said. "And since you are awake so late, I made a batch of sweet bread last night. Here, take a few slices."

She appeared with a tray of pumpkin bread. "It has pecans in it. Tell me how you like it."

Harold took a slice of pumpkin bread and stuffed it in his mouth, tipping his hat to her. "Thank you, ma'am, but I do have to go. No one is escaping tonight, not on my watch."

Mrs. Porter stepped back in surprise. "Oh, I'm sorry. I didn't mean to cause trouble."

"You didn't, ma'am. I just have my job to do," Harold said.

"Well, do your job," she said. "I'm going back to bed."

Harold didn't move. He stared at Mrs. Porter and grew suspicious. Everything seemed too casual. It was after midnight, and Mrs. Porter was more interested in serving sweet bread than finding out who was prowling around in her barn.

"Mrs. Porter!" Harold shouted.

"Yes?"

"Can you wake Joseph up? I need to talk to him."

Mrs. Porter hesitated.

"He is in bed asleep, isn't he?" Harold asked.

"I don't see how he could still be asleep, with all this racket going on," she said. "But I'll get him."

Five minutes passed, and she did not return. Harold grew impatient. His heart pounded, and hot anger swept over him.

"You are making a fool of me," he hissed.

He opened the back door and slammed it so hard the windows rattled.

"Mrs. Porter! Where is Joseph?"

"Oh, I'm sorry to keep you waiting," she said, leaning out the door. "I looked all over for him. I forgot. He's spending the night with his older brother. You can talk to him in the morning. Good night, and try not to slam the door again."

"I know where Joseph is," Harold shouted. "He's going to help his father escape!"

Harold rounded the house and dashed to the road, clutching his shotgun in front of him. As he stepped from the trees and into the moonlight, his hat fluttered and flew from his head. He grabbed for it—missed— then turned his total attention to Joseph, Mr. Porter, and THE BIG ESCAPE.

Joseph watched from the roadside bushes. When

Harold's hat flew from his head, Joseph jumped from the shadows and plucked it from the ground.

This might come in handy, he thought.

Joseph darted for the woods and made his own path as he ran. He dodged low-hanging branches and leapt over fallen trees. He crawled under vines and scrambled to his feet. He ran for fear and he ran for joy—fear for his father and joy that he would soon be home.

Out of breath from running, Joseph flopped to the ground and leaned against a stout tree stump. The barn wall was fifteen feet in front of him. On the other side of the wall sat his father, waiting for his nightly drink of water.

Harold will be here soon, thought Joseph. He crept to the barn and put his ear against the wooden planks. No sound. An owl flew from the rafter overhead.

"Hooooo!" The scream was long and sharp. He heard his father move.

Joseph knocked on the wall. "Dad," he whispered.

His father knocked from the other side, signaling that all was safe.

"Come in, Joseph."

"Dad, can you hear me?"

"Yes. Come around to the door, son. No one is here but us."

"Dad, Harold is on his way. He has a shotgun, and he'll be here any minute."

"Are you sure?"

"Yes, Dad. He's been watching the house. He might do something. Something he can brag about later. I'm scared!"

"Son, stay where you are. Don't let him see you, whatever you do. I will be very careful. I promise."

"Who are you talking to?" Harold shouted, stepping through the barn door, huffing and puffing and dragging his shotgun behind him.

CHAPTER 23

Shot in the Dark

"Hello, Harold," said Mr. Porter. "You caught me. I was talking to myself again. I've been doing it for several days now. Don't tell Mrs. Porter. It'll make her worry."

Harold paused for a long moment, staring hard at Mr. Porter. "Where's Joseph?" he asked.

"I'm guessing he's in bed by now," Mr. Porter said.

"No, he's not in bed. I was sent by Mr. Bledsoe to keep an eye on your house, and I've been doing just that. Every night. And tonight, I saw Joseph leaving the house."

Mr. Porter sat without speaking.

"Where is he, Mr. Porter? I have to tell Mr. Bledsoe, you know." Harold walked slowly past the stalls. He lifted a lantern from a nail on the wall and lit the wick. Yellow light exploded the darkness.

The lantern swung at his knees, casting giant shadows

of horses on the ceiling of the barn. A horse stomped and whinnied. Harold raised his shotgun to his shoulder as he approached the jail.

Mr. Porter moved to the rear of his tiny cell. "Harold," he said in a quiet voice, "there is no one here. Just you and me. See for yourself."

Harold peered through the steel bars. Other than a rolled-up blanket and a wooden bucket, the cell was empty.

"Nobody but me. Let Mr. Bledsoe sleep. He wouldn't like it, you waking him up for no good reason," Mr. Porter said, running his hand through his hair. "I could use some sleep myself."

Harold hesitated. He didn't know what to believe. He cast a long look at Mr. Porter. "This isn't over with yet," he said through clenched teeth. "Mr. Bledsoe will back me up, whatever I do. He already told me. I could kill you right now and claim you tried to escape."

As if in response to Harold's threat, a heavy pounding shook the barn door. Harold put down the lantern and ran to the door. He spotted someone crouching in the nearby woods, his hat hiding his face.

"It's time to pay up," Harold whispered.

He lifted his shotgun and took aim. The shotgun blast sent the hat soaring twenty feet into the woods. Alarmed by the blast, the forest came alive. Birds flew from the treetops, and possums, squirrels, and foxes all ran for cover.

Harold cocked his head, uncertain if his shot had hit anyone. He saw the hat fly, but he'd expected to hear a groan, a gasp of pain, something at least from Joseph.

"What was that?" shouted Mr. Porter.

"I'll know as soon as I drag the body to the light," said Harold. He took the lantern and crept slowly toward the trees.

When he heard the shotgun blast, Bledsoe was standing on his back porch, smoking his pipe before retiring. He grabbed his own gun and hurried to the barn, stopping en route at the barracks where the young guards slept.

"To the barn! Quick!" he yelled, pounding his fist on the door.

Bledsoe arrived just as Harold was entering the woods.

"Who fired the shot?" Bledsoe demanded.

"I did, Mr. Bledsoe," said Harold. His eyes grew large, and he stood at attention, seeing the flurry of action caused by his firing at Joseph.

Guards were gathering. Light blinked on in windows all over the plantation. While Zeke hurried to the barn, Joseph's mother fell to her knees in prayer.

"What were you aiming at?" Bledsoe asked.

"Joseph Porter," said Harold. "He was trying to break his father out, but I got him."

"Bring him to me!" said Bledsoe.

"Yes, sir!" Harold said proudly. While everyone waited, Harold entered the woods, his shotgun on his hip. Bledsoe held the lantern high.

"I've got his hat," Harold hollered.

"Is there blood on the hat?" asked Bledsoe.

Harold didn't reply. He stepped from the woods and handed Bledsoe the hat. The top of the hat was blown away. The jagged edge of the cloth was framed in powder burns.

"No one could have survived this," Bledsoe said quietly.

"That's what I was thinking!" said Harold. "I killed him!"

"Unless he wasn't wearing the hat," Bledsoe said, staring at Harold. "Maybe the hat was hanging from a tree limb."

"No, sir," Harold insisted. Then he squinted his eyes at the hat and took a step backward. He grimaced and hung his head.

"Mr. Bledsoe," he said, "that's my hat. I lost it on the way here. Joseph must have stolen it."

"Not another word," Bledsoe said. "Do you know

the trouble you've caused, Harold? Come see me in the morning."

Harold started to speak, but Bledsoe held up his hand to silence him.

"Everyone can go home now," he said. "We have a hard day ahead of us tomorrow. Cotton won't pick itself. And I will have some explaining to do at the plantation house," he added, looking at Harold.

During the commotion, Mr. Porter sat at the back of his cell. Joseph leaned against the outside wall, six inches away. When he heard Bledsoe's voice, Mr. Porter said, "Son, be as quiet as you can. Get yourself home."

"Yes, Dad. I love you. I'll see you tomorrow."

Joseph slipped into the shadowy woods and hurried home. He met his mother on the back porch.

"Everything is fine, Mother," he said. "Dad is safe. Harold won't be bothering us for a while."

———

From the Choctaw side, Koi Losa and Lil Mo saw the lights and heard the shotgun. They awakened Funi Man, and the three kept watch on the banks of Bok Chitto till the morning sun sent golden rays over the water.

CHAPTER 24

Father and Son

Early the next morning, Bledsoe walked from the cotton fields to the plantation house. He knew that Mr. Kendall, the plantation owner, would be on the balcony, enjoying his morning coffee and watching the sun rise.

"Did the gunfire wake you up last night?" he asked, removing his hat and bowing his head to Mr. Kendall.

"Yes," said Mr. Kendall. He gazed over the balcony rail as he spoke. When he turned slowly, Bledsoe saw that he was angry. "You have something to tell me about last night?" Mr. Kendall asked.

"Yes," said Bledsoe. "I wanted to make certain the field workers were not involved before I reported to you."

"All seems normal in the fields," said Mr. Kendall.

"Yes. Of course, everyone heard the shot, but no one was injured or tried to escape."

"You have found the shooter, then?"

"Yes," said Bledsoe. "Harold, one of my guards."

"The young and fiery-tempered one, am I correct?"

"Yes, Harold is sometimes quick to anger. I have him guarding the Porter family."

"The Porters?"

"Yes. Porter was the head guard who allowed the slaves to cross the river."

"So you are keeping watch on the family?"

"I thought it wise, sir," Bledsoe replied.

"Mr. Porter, correct me if I am wrong, has been in our service for most of his life?"

"Yes, since he was a young man himself. He has his own family now."

"Do you suspect he was somehow aligned with the slaves who escaped?"

"No," said Bledsoe. "But he displayed cowardice. He could have shot at least one, as a sign to the others. They would have stopped to save one of their own."

"Earlier, you reported that the Choctaws crossed the river and helped in the escape."

"Yes, that is what was told to me."

"So a shot from Mr. Porter might very well have started a war with the Choctaws. A war, I might remind you, we are not prepared to fight."

Bledsoe felt the anger growing in his chest. He knew

his men could destroy the Choctaw town if given the chance. He also knew better than to say it.

"Tell me about the shot," said Mr. Kendall. "I was told it came from the barn. If Harold was guarding the Porters, what was he doing in the barn?"

"Mr. Porter is there, sir. I am keeping him in the jail till we decide what punishment is best for him."

"The slave jail, where we keep runaways? Your most trusted guard, the man you sent to catch the escaping family? You have him in the slave jail?"

"Yes."

"Since the night of the escape, more than a week ago?"

"Yes," said Bledsoe. He raised his eyes to meet Mr. Kendall's. "He has been kept under watch. Harold reported seeing his son leave the house last night. He feared he was trying to help his father escape."

"And he fired the shot at the boy?" asked Mr. Kendall.

"Yes, into the woods where the Porter boy was spotted, by the barn."

"Was the boy injured?

"No, he was not hit."

"Mr. Bledsoe, tell me the truth about last night. What happened?"

"Harold heard something moving at the rear of the Porter house. He followed what he thought was Joseph, the Porter boy, to the barn. Harold saw a hat and fired at it."

"It was the Porter boy's hat?" Mr. Kendall asked.

"No. The hat belonged to Harold. He had lost it on the way to the barn."

"So," said Mr. Kendall, "you are telling me the plantation was awakened last night when one of your guards shot at his own hat? Is that what I am hearing?"

"He's a young man. He makes mistakes."

"Mr. Bledsoe, I think the biggest mistake was made by you. A loyal guard, an employee of mine for more than forty years, made a decision that can be questioned. But no shots were fired. No armies are gathering. And now you have a very suspect young man guarding him? You are keeping him in a jail meant for slaves?"

Bledsoe did not reply.

"I think you have jailed the wrong man," Mr. Kendall said. "Set him free this morning. Return him to the fields, to his old job."

"Yes, sir," Bledsoe said. His face was tight, and his heart pounded in his chest.

"And one more thing, Mr. Bledsoe."

"Yes. Will there be anything else?" asked Bledsoe.

Mr. Kendall noted Bledsoe's tone of sarcasm and raised his eyebrows. "Yes," he said. "There will be something else. I do not want Porter to be punished in any way, ever again, for his possible mistake. Do you understand me?"

"I do," said Bledsoe.

"Tell Porter I would like to see him at the end of the week."

"Mr. Kendall, sir, that is not necessary. He will receive no punishment. I assure you."

"Good," said Mr. Kendall. "Then my meeting with him will be brief. Saturday evening. Let him know I will see him then. Here, on the balcony."

CHAPTER 25

Zeke and His Father

Bledsoe left the meeting in a state of fury. He found Harold at the barracks, waiting for his orders for the day.

"You are to return to the fields. No more watching the Porter house," Bledsoe told him.

"Mr. Bledsoe, I know it was Joseph. I should have killed him long ago."

"Mr. Kendall sees things otherwise," said Bledsoe. "At least for now. You were a fool to shoot at nothing but a hat hanging from a tree. Your actions have resulted in Porter going free."

"Free! They're letting that coward go?"

"Yes," Bledsoe said. "And if you so much as speak to him or any of his family, you will answer to me. You have caused enough trouble for now."

He turned to leave, then remembered his real purpose

in coming. "Harold," he said. "I need your gun."

"Why?"

"You will be an overseer only, at least till we can determine if you can be trusted with a shotgun. Now, give it to me."

Harold took the shotgun from a trunk by his bed. He clenched his teeth tight and tried to fight back the tears. When Bledsoe was gone, he spat on the floor.

"You will pay for this, Joseph," he said to himself. "You and your family. They won't keep my gun from me forever."

———

Bledsoe made his way to the cotton fields and found Zeke standing guard over the field workers, his shotgun over his shoulder.

"Zeke, your father is taking back his old job. Here is the key to his leg chain," Bledsoe said, tossing the key to Zeke. "I need you to take him home. Tell him to report to work tomorrow morning."

"My father? So you are letting him out of jail?"

"*I* am not letting your father out of jail. I'm following the orders from the main house. Mr. Kendall thinks he can be trusted. More than me, apparently."

Bledsoe made no attempt to hide his anger. He let the

fire show in his eyes as he whispered, "This affair is not over yet. Go now. I'll take over here till after lunch."

Trying to hide his joy, Zeke hurried to the barn.

"Good news," he said, approaching his father's cell. "You're going home. Bledsoe said for you to report to work tomorrow morning."

"Zeke! I can't believe this is happening," Mr. Porter said, standing and brushing the sawdust from his pants. "I thought I might never get out of here alive."

"No more slipping you dinner after dark," said Zeke. "We can have a real family meal tonight."

"Oh, son, your mother will be so happy. I'm sure she's been crying herself to sleep every night. You know how much she worries."

Zeke unlocked the chain and gripped his father's elbow. "Take it easy, Dad. One step at a time. It's been a long time since you walked."

They left the barn and Mr. Porter shielded his eyes from the bright morning sun. "What a blessing!" he said. "I've never been so happy to be blinded by the sunlight."

They walked in silence till they came to the fields. The field workers were tossing cotton bolls into their shoulder bags. When they saw Mr. Porter, they stood. Every worker, every man and every woman, young and old, they all stood and bowed their heads as Mr. Porter passed.

Soon the workers leaned and knelt and returned to

their work, but as they disappeared into the thick rows of cotton, a new sound lifted through the air. A soft hymn, sung by the field workers, moved up and down the cotton rows, rose to the treetops, and was heard as far away as Choctaw town.

> *I am bound for the promised land,*
> *I am bound for the promised land,*
> *O, who will come and go with me?*
> *I am bound for the promised land.*

Lil Mo and Koi Losa heard the song. They lifted their necks above the tree limbs and saw Mr. Porter walking home in the distance, his head bowed but his spirit lifted.

"Yes," whispered Lil Mo.

"Yakoke!" said Koi Losa.

CHAPTER 26

Ofijo's First Day Home

1808, City of Bok Chitto, Choctaw Nation

Every morning, just before sunrise, Funi Man appeared at the lean-to, cradling Ofijo in his arms. Ofijo was growing quickly. He was a happy pup, a reddish-brown ball of bouncing fur. He wagged his tail when he spotted Lil Mo, then crawled onto his chest and licked his cheeks.

"You're his best buddy," said Funi Man.

Every day Lil Mo asked the same question.

"Why can't I see where Ofijo lives?"

And every day Funi Man gave the same answer.

"He lives with his new mother till he is old enough to stay with you, Lil Mo. That's all you need to know. I don't want you running around getting yourself in trouble."

"I wouldn't do that!" said Lil Mo.

Funi Man lifted his eyebrows. "Yeah, Lil Mo. You never get in trouble. But the next time you do, you'll have a new friend to protect you."

"You mean Ofijo, don't you?" Lil Mo asked.

"Yes. If you treat him like family, Ofijo will always be there when you need him," said Funi Man. "He might even save your life someday."

Lil Mo smiled and rubbed Ofijo's ears. "I like that. Ofijo saving my life! You would do that for me, wouldn't you, Ofijo?"

"Ruff, ruff," said Ofijo, wagging his tail.

One morning Funi Man and Ofijo appeared long before sunrise. Funi Man slipped into the lean-to and knelt beside Lil Mo. "Time to wake up," he whispered. "I brought a friend who says he's ready to live here."

Lil Mo opened his eyes and laughed quietly.

"Ofijo," he said. "Good morning to you."

Ofijo jumped to the ground and yelped, "Rrrufff!"

"Today is the day?" asked Lil Mo. "He can stay with me all the time?"

"He is old enough now," Funi Man said. "Ofijo is now part of the Lil Mo clan."

"Can I take him for a walk?"

"Whatever you want to do," said Funi Man. "He's your friend now."

Once outside, Ofijo watered the trunk of the nearby cypress tree.

"Good boy!" said Lil Mo.

Breakfast chores were beginning in the lean-to. While his father lit the fire, Lil Mo gathered twigs and firewood, with Ofijo by his side. Angel peeled corncobs and scraped kernels into the pot. Soon water was boiling for coffee, and corn soup was boiling in the pot. The aroma of soup filled the tiny lean-to.

"Smells good in here," said Funi Man.

"I made enough for you, so stay for breakfast," Treda said. "We even have an extra bowl."

"How can I turn down breakfast with my favorite family in town?" Funi Man asked. He took his place in the family circle and soon dipped his spoon in the sweet corn pashofa. "Mmm," he whispered, nodding at Treda.

But during the meal Funi Man spoke not a word.

"Why are you being so quiet, Funi Man?" Lil Mo asked.

"I have some wonderful news, and I've been waiting for the perfect moment to tell you," said Funi Man.

"How about now?" Lil Mo said.

"Son," said Lavester, "it's time to listen."

"Thank you, Lavester," Funi Man said. "You and Treda are okla chukma. Good people. We Choctaws have welcomed a family of okla chukma to our town."

"Thank you. Yakoke," said Treda.

"You seem comfortable here in your lean-to," Funi Man said, "but you need a home. This lean-to has served a good purpose. But you no longer need to stay hidden. The council met yesterday, and every member agreed. You are Choctaws now. They decided you need a home."

Treda and Lavester looked at each other.

"I would like you to live close to me," Funi Man said. "I have a large piece of land, more than I need. My mother and father lived there for most of their lives. They are gone now, and their old house is empty. I would be proud to have you live in my parents' old house."

Lavester stood slowly. From where she sat, Treda stared at the roof. The morning sun, one golden ray at a time, slipped through the cracks of the cedar branches. The lean-to floated in a cloud of light. Lavester and Treda knew they were entering a world they never knew existed. They had dreamed of freedom, but they never thought they could have their own home.

"The soil is rich. A spring of cool water bubbles up from the ground," Funi Man said. "You can have your own plot for a garden. You can help in the Choctaw corn-field and share the crop."

Lavester took a deep breath. Fat tears flowed from his tight-shut eyes. He shook all over. Treda stood behind him and wrapped her arms around his chest.

"One other thing," said Funi Man. "You will need

a pony to help with the work. I want to give you one of mine."

"A Choctaw pony!" Lil Mo said, then clamped his hand over his mouth.

"That's hoke, son," his mother said, wiping her eyes. "We should be happy."

"I'll leave you now," Funi Man said. "We can see the old house this afternoon. It needs work, but you will have plenty of help." He ducked under the roof of the lean-to and was gone.

Lil Mo had seen his parents happy before, but never like this. He stood in the doorway and stared. Lavester took Treda by the waist and spun her around. Not once, but several times, over and over. When she grew dizzy and fell, he caught her with his strong right arm and lifted her over his head.

"Lavester!" Treda shouted. "PUT . . . ME . . . DOWN!" She laughed so hard she could barely spit out the words.

When his mother and father started kissing and rubbing noses, Lil Mo had seen enough. He stepped outside, shaking his head.

"I'm just glad Martha Tom is not here to see this," he said to himself—or so he thought.

Martha Tom was waiting for him by the big oak tree. "See what?" she asked.

"Nothing," said Lil Mo. "I just caught a raccoon with

my bare hands, but I decided to let him go."

"Too bad," said Martha Tom. "Ofijo needs a smart friend to play with, and even a raccoon is smarter than you."

"You're not nice to me," Lil Mo said.

"You never tell me the truth," Martha Tom replied.

Lil Mo had to agree she was right. He didn't mind this little fuss with Martha Tom, as long as she didn't see his parents rubbing noses.

"Yuck!" he said out loud, remembering.

"Yuck to you, Lil Mo," Martha Tom said, walking away.

CHAPTER 27

A New Home for Lil Mo's Family

Two hours later, Funi Man stood outside the lean-to and announced, "I think it's time to see your new home."

"We are ready," Lavester said. "This day is very special for my family."

Funi Man took the lead, beaming with pride. "You'll be living in my parents' old home," he said. "It'll be nice to see children play in the yard I grew up in!"

As they left the lean-to, Lil Mo saw Martha Tom, sitting in the shade by the river. *She sure is hanging around a lot these days,* he thought.

During the walk, she snuck up behind him and tapped him on the shoulder. He turned around, and Martha Tom looked at him without saying a word.

"Why are you acting so strange?" he asked. "Are you feeling hoke?"

"No," said Martha Tom. "I am not hoke. I heard all about your new home."

"So that's what you're mad about?"

"That's not funny," she said. "You know what I'm talking about."

"Maybe you better explain to Lil Mo. He's not as smart as he looks."

Martha Tom stopped. She folded her arms and stared at Lil Mo. "I thought we were friends," she said.

"We are friends! Why are you saying that?"

"You could have asked me to see your new home."

"Oh," Lil Mo said. "You want to go with us?"

"If you don't want me along, I don't want to go."

"Martha Tom, you are my almost best friend in the world. Yes, I want you to see our new home."

"Hmpf," said Martha Tom. "You could have asked."

Lil Mo was confused. He stepped back and looked at Martha Tom. *I should say something,* he thought. "I will be a better friend," he finally said.

"That's hoke," said Martha Tom, and they walked without speaking for the next half-mile.

As the group reached the crest of a small knoll, Martha Tom turned around and dashed down the hill. "Chi pisa la chike," she said over her shoulder.

"That means 'good-bye,'" said Funi Man, "but I don't think she wants to say good-bye to you." He smiled, shook his head, and pointed to his cabin below. "That's my place. I've been there for forty-some years now, just me and whatever crawls through my window."

"So nobody can come see you unless they crawl through your window?" Lil Mo asked. "That's funny!"

"Yeah," said Funi Man, with his rolling-eyes smile. "That's funny. And Treda, Lavester," he continued, pointing to a clump of elms, "that cabin through the trees, that will be your new home for as long as you want to live next door to me."

"I think that's gonna be a long time, my friend," said Lavester.

For the next hour Lil Mo and his family explored their new home. Everyone had the same thought.

It's been a long time since anyone lived here!

Small trees sprouted through the floor, and birds flew in and out of the windows. The porch was covered with tall weeds, and the roof had fallen in on the back half of the house.

Lavester approached Lil Mo and lifted him from the ground. "Son," he said, "we have our work cut out for us. You and I, Lil Mo, will build a home for our family. What do you think about that?"

"Hoke, Papa," Lil Mo replied, relieved when his father set him on the ground. "So this is really our house, nobody else's?"

"That's right, son."

"And nobody, not Bledsoe or anybody, can tell us what to do?"

"That's right, son."

"I really like that, Papa, that nobody can tell me what to do."

Funi Man gave him a look that said, *I know what you're thinking, Lil Mo, but don't say it.*

Lil Mo laughed. "When do we start, Papa?" he asked.

"Well, maybe we can start by clearing these weeds from the porch."

"Be right back," said Funi Man. "Come on, Lil Mo!" They soon returned, carrying a shovel and three hoes. He passed them out, and everyone went to work. They pulled rotten boards from the porch, twice disturbing sleeping rattlesnakes.

"Yow!" yelled Lil Mo.

"Whatever you do," Funi Man said, "don't strike those rattlers. You remember the lesson."

"I won't," said Lil Mo. "They surprised me, that's all."

"Remember, we are the ones disturbing their home. At least, that's how they see it."

Lil Mo shook his head and tried his best not to laugh.

Funi Man has to be the funniest man alive, he thought. *I could get swallowed by the biggest snake in the world, and Funi Man would hope I didn't choke the snake!*

Soon Funi Man led Angel and Treda to his house, and they returned with a bucket of water and bits of old, worn-out clothing. While the men worked on the porch and floor, Angel and Treda scrubbed and washed the cabin walls.

Just before sunset, Funi Man built a fire in front of the house. Martha Tom and her mother Ella appeared, carrying bowls and pots and everything needed for a Choctaw feast: six skinned squirrels, two dozen fresh-picked corn-cobs, blackberries and fresh cream, and a bag filled with roots and herbs for flavoring.

Lil Mo watched with surprise as Funi Man poked a sharp stick through a skinned squirrel and held it over the fire. The squirrel sizzled and smoked. Juice dripped over the flames, sending sparks popping on anyone sitting too close.

"Funi Man," said Lil Mo, "I thought they call you Squirrel Man. That's your Choctaw name, right?"

"That's right," Funi Man said.

"Hoke. Then why are you cooking squirrels?"

"Lil Mo," he said, "I am called Funi Man—Squirrel Man—because I know squirrels. I know how to find them, how to hunt them, and how to cook them."

"I thought you were their friend."

"I am their friend," Funi Man replied. "But that doesn't mean I won't feed my family, my Choctaw family. I say my prayers for the squirrels. I thank them for the gift of good meat. I respect the squirrels, and they respect me."

"Sometimes I don't understand this Choctaw way of thinking," said Lil Mo.

Lavester put his bowl down and looked at Lil Mo. He gestured to the house and to the open fields.

"But I like it, and I am thankful," Lil Mo added.

His father nodded and gave him a *that's better, son* look.

"Wonder where Koi Losa is?" Lil Mo asked Funi Man.

"Oh, he is probably doing what he does best," said Funi Man.

"Keeping an eye out for troublemakers?" asked Lil Mo.

"Yes, Lil Mo. We want nothing to spoil this day for your family."

Koi Losa was keeping watch, just as Funi Man had asked him to.

CHAPTER 28

The Bone Pickers

One week later

With a roof overhead and a floor underfoot, Lil Mo's family settled into a routine. Lavester and Lil Mo worked in the Choctaw cornfield, while Treda and Angel scrubbed and cleaned every corner of the house.

One morning, long before sunrise, Ofijo jumped on Lil Mo's belly, ready for the day to begin. He whined and licked his good friend's face to wake him.

"Good morning," Lil Mo said. "Onnahinli chukma." He wanted Ofijo to learn Choctaw, too.

Ofijo didn't wait for Lil Mo to get up. He dashed out the door, tumbled over a corncob, and rolled to his feet.

When Lil Mo joined him, Ofijo was bouncing up and down by his food dish.

"Too early for breakfast," Lil Mo said. "Let's take a walk." He looked to the pine thicket north of the cornfield.

"We've never gone this way," he said. He broke into a run. Ofijo barked and scrambled to keep up. As they neared the trees, rolling clouds darkened the sky. A half-mile from the house, Lil Mo felt the first raindrop splatter on his cheek.

"Uh-oh. I think we're walking into a storm." He hurried to the trees and ducked under a roof of low-hanging pine branches. "Come on, Ofijo!" he called out.

He scooped up his pup and ran his hand across Ofijo's wet back. He was considering making a run for home before the full storm hit, when he saw it—the green glow of the Bohpoli lantern. Funi Man had told him stories of the Bohpoli.

"The Bohpoli!" he shouted. "Ofijo, you want to meet the Bohpoli?"

"Ruff, ruff!"

"Yeah, I thought so," he said. "Let's go!"

Soon he and Ofijo were darting through pine trees and leaping over fallen logs, chasing the Bohpoli lantern.

Thunder crashed, and a bolt of lightning hit a nearby tree, knocking Lil Mo to the ground. He rose slowly. The green light flickered in the silvery rain.

Lil Mo realized he was entering the world of the Bohpoli and leaving his own. The light glowed brightest near a Choctaw mound, a small, round-topped hill. Lil Mo slowed down to catch his breath as they approached the mound.

The lantern circled the mound, and Lil Mo followed. On the backside of the grassy hill, Lil Mo lost the light, but only for a moment. A flickering caught his eye from deep in the woods. For another half hour, he and Ofijo followed the Bohpoli lantern. The rain fell heavy and cold, and they were both soaked.

"Maybe a walk in a thunderstorm wasn't such a good idea," Lil Mo said.

Suddenly the green light burst into flames, only a few feet in front of him. Lil Mo covered his eyes and inched forward with tiny steps.

"Where are you?" he whispered.

Just as quickly as it appeared, the light vanished. Lil Mo stood at the door of an old log house. The roof was made of dried and cracked palmetto leaves.

"You're a long way from home," said a voice.

Lil Mo jumped. "Oh! Yes, I'm sorry. Me and my dog were just walking." He picked up Ofijo and held him close to his chest. Ofijo shivered from the cold.

"You don't have to stand in the rain," said the voice, coming from inside. "We don't have visitors every day."

"We never have visitors!" said another voice.

"Don't be scared," said the first voice. An elderly woman appeared at the door. Her hair was white and tied in a tight bun at the back of her head. She wore a loose-hanging white dress

I have never seen anybody this old, thought Lil Mo. The woman stooped when she walked. Skin hung from the bones of her face. Her eyebrows were thick and bushy.

She took Lil Mo by the arm and led him through a narrow door. Embers glowed from a small stone fireplace on the back wall. The logs hissed and crackled as raindrops fell down the chimney. The room smelled of smoke—and something else.

Lil Mo felt uncomfortable. Something was not right about this place. The other woman sat on a cypress log in a dark corner, away from the fire. A blanket was draped over her shoulders, and she kept her back turned to Lil Mo.

She doesn't want me here, Lil Mo thought.

"I should go now," he said. "My dog and I will be hoke."

At that moment, Ofijo wiggled free and plopped onto the dirt floor. He scampered across the room to the darkest corner. The unseen woman slapped him with her blanket, and Ofijo barked and growled in a way Lil Mo had never heard.

"Ofi okpulo!" the woman said, stomping the floor. "Bad dog!"

"I'm sorry," Lil Mo said, running for Ofijo. "He's just a puppy. He doesn't know any better." As he scooped Ofijo into his arms, Lil Mo saw what gave this house the heavy stench. He moved slowly to the door.

The women stared at each other, waiting for Lil Mo to speak. Lil Mo pretended to see nothing unusual. He tried to smile, but the thick smoke and the horrible smell were too much for him. He shook his head, but the image of what he had seen would not go away.

The old woman in the shadows was hunched over a pile of bones. With her long black fingernails, she was peeling wrinkled skin from the bones and stacking them in the corner.

Lil Mo eased his way, one backward step at a time, to the front door. His eyes stayed glued to the woman who had led him into the house, in case she tried to grab him.

Ofijo growled. Lil Mo felt his heart thumping in his chest. The women made no move to stop him. When Lil Mo reached the door, he turned to run.

He never made it out the door. He bumped into another woman, a large woman, who wrapped her strong arms around him.

CHAPTER 29

Friends Ever After

"Let me go!" Lil Mo hollered.

"Lil Mo," the woman said, "you don't have to be afraid of me." Lil Mo looked into the friendly, smiling face of Shonti.

"You must be lost," Shonti said, laughing and shaking her head. "Wait till Funi Man hears about this! Looks like you've met my friends."

"He was walking around in the pouring-down rain," said the friendly woman. "I took him in to dry off, but he didn't want to stay."

"He was poking around where he had no business," said the woman in the corner, with her back still turned.

"Maybe we should just get to know each other," Shonti said. "Lil Mo, these women are my friends. And you can't go outside. It's still raining."

Lil Mo looked to Shonti, pleading, *"No!"* He held Ofijo tight to his chest.

"Lil Mo," Shonti asked, "hasn't Funi Man been teaching you about Choctaw ways?"

"Yes, but he didn't tell me anything about this," Lil Mo said. Ofijo barked and growled as the grouchy woman flung off her blanket and stood up.

"You better teach that dog of yours some manners," she said. "I have a dog of my own." She pulled aside a dark curtain, revealing a small closet.

Stretched across the floor of the closet lay the largest dog Lil Mo had ever seen. He was black as night with droopy eyes and small, pointed ears. He yawned and scratched his thin tail across the dirt floor.

Lil Mo stared as the dog lifted his head and looked around the room. Drool dripped from his jowls. His nose twitched as he sniffed the air. Lil Mo wrapped both arms around Ofijo, hoping the big dog wouldn't see him.

But Ofijo saw the big dog.

He squirmed and wriggled his way free. Before Lil Mo could stop him, Ofijo jumped to the floor and ran to the closet. He leapt high and sailed through the open door, landing against the big dog's chest.

The dog looked surprised. He uttered a deep, low bark and shook his head. Dog drool splattered from his mouth and covered Ofijo. Ofijo whined and ran his paws across his face. Lil Mo expected the big dog to open his mouth and swallow Ofijo.

"Ofijo, meet Little Bear," Shonti said. Lil Mo stared up at Shonti. He could not believe her friendly tone, her smiling face.

"'Ofijo, meet Little Bear'?" he repeated. "How can you be smiling?" He struggled to free himself—to rescue Ofijo—but Shonti held him tight.

Lil Mo watched as Little Bear slapped a big paw over Ofijo, completely covering everything but his tail. Lil Mo held his breath, but Shonti seemed unconcerned. When Ofijo wagged his tail, Lil Mo relaxed.

Little Bear lifted his paw and leaned back to get a good look at Ofijo. With a low growl, he opened his enormous mouth and wrapped his jowls around the squiggly pup.

Ofijo disappeared inside Little Bear's mouth!

"Lil Mo," said Shonti, "you must give Little Bear a chance."

"'Give Little Bear a chance'?!" shouted Lil Mo. "He is eating Ofijo!"

Little Bear lifted Ofijo and tossed his head back and forth, then dropped him to the floor.

Ofijo barked and wagged his tail faster. He ran at Little Bear, barking and saying in dogtalk, "Let's do that again!"

"See, Lil Mo," Shonti said. "Little Bear is Ofijo's friend. You must stop judging everybody before you know them."

"Sorry," said Lil Mo. "I guess okla chukma is about dogs, too."

"Yes, Lil Mo. Okla chukma, good people, come in all shapes and sizes and colors. Even dogs!" She laughed and hugged him close. Lil Mo stood still and let her hold him, but he didn't like it.

Now I know why Ofijo tries to jump when I hold him tight, he thought. Like many of his thoughts where grown-ups were concerned, he had learned not to say them out loud.

By now Ofijo and Little Bear were best buddies. Ofijo was jumping on Little Bear's back and crawling all over him. Little Bear shook his back, slapped his huge paw on Ofijo, and let him wriggle free.

"Hoke," Shonti said. "Now that Little Bear and Ofijo are friends, you can meet my friends, Bishkoko and Tilly. Ladies, this is Lil Mo. He is with the family you have heard so much about lately, the one that crossed the river."

CHAPTER 30

Martha Tom and the Bone Pickers

Ofijo played with his new friend, Little Bear, while Shonti served potatoes with pork and boiled corn bread. Bishkoko and Tilly ate quietly by the fire, and Lil Mo sat near the door.

Just in case I need to run, he thought. He dove into his food like he had not eaten all day, because of course he had not.

After breakfast Shonti said, "Lil Mo, your clothes are wet. You must be cold. Why don't you step behind the curtain and hand me your clothes? I'll dry them over the fire."

Lil Mo didn't like the idea of taking his clothes off in this house of bones, but he was still shivering from the cold rain. He stepped behind the curtain, tossed his pants and shirt over the curtain rod, and sat in the tiny space with Ofijo and Little Bear.

Peeping through the curtains, Lil Mo saw Shonti take his clothes and hang them over a branch before moving it to the fire. Then he saw something in the doorway that took his breath away.

"No!" he whispered. "Please don't let her know I am here. Please!"

Martha Tom stood at the door.

"Halito," she said. "I am sorry to be so late. I waited till the rain slacked up."

"That's hoke," said Shonti. "Just leave the basket by the fire here. We have already eaten."

Martha Tom entered the house and stood next to Shonti. She wrapped her arms around herself and shivered. "Brrrr! It is so cold."

Lil Mo hid behind Little Bear. *What if she opens the curtain?*

"Where is Little Bear?" Martha Tom asked.

No! thought Lil Mo. *She's going to look for Little Bear! I am dead! Naked and dead!*

But Martha Tom did not look behind the curtain. She stayed by the warmth of the fire.

"Oh, he's still sleeping," said Shonti.

Yes! Shonti is protecting me! thought Lil Mo.

"He has a new friend," said Shonti.

No! Don't tell her about Ofijo! She will ask how Ofijo got here!

Shonti did not tell Martha Tom about Ofijo. She didn't have to tell her. Ofijo heard her voice and dashed from the curtained corner, jumping and yelping at Martha Tom's feet.

"Hello, Ofijo!" said Martha Tom. "How did you get here?"

Lil Mo flung himself against the wall in terror.

Shonti is smart, he thought. *Really smart. She can make up a simple story. Yes, Shonti will protect me.*

"Lil Mo brought him," Shonti said. "He's standing behind the curtain, in Little Bear's corner. But it's probably best if you don't see him now, since I'm drying his clothes."

Hoke, thought Lil Mo. *All is not lost. These sweet ladies will know a painless way to kill me. They will know exactly how to pick the flesh from my bones. I will be dead and buried and never have to see Martha Tom again!*

Lil Mo heard somebody laugh. No, he heard *several* somebodies laugh.

"Lil Mo," said Martha Tom, in a singsong voice, "come out, come out, wherever you are!"

"Lil Mo left," said Lil Mo. "He crawled out the window and drowned in the swamp. So don't worry about Lil Mo anymore. Just be nice and go home."

"There's no window in Little Bear's room," said Bishkoko. More laughter, louder this time.

"Can everybody just go away?" Lil Mo asked. "Please?"

"Lil Mo," Shonti said, "don't be so silly! Your clothes are dry. Martha Tom, will you bring Lil Mo his clothes?"

"Shonti!" Lil Mo yelled.

Still more laughter, louder than ever.

"Only joking," Shonti said. "Here!" Lil Mo's clothes appeared over the curtain. "My goodness, you sure are acting like a scared little boy."

"That's because I am one!" said Lil Mo.

———

Later, after the sky cleared, Martha Tom led Lil Mo on a shortcut home. "Nobody ever uses this road," she said. "Well, almost never."

"Why is it here?" Lil Mo asked.

"Sometimes wagons carry things to the ladies," Martha Tom said, in a voice so soft he barely heard her.

"Are you going to tell me about what I saw? Why that old woman in the corner was picking the flesh from bones? They looked like human bones." Lil Mo stopped walking and waited for Martha Tom to meet his eyes.

"They were," said Martha Tom. "Lil Mo, Funi Man has already told you some Choctaw ways. But he hasn't told you everything."

"You don't have to convince me of that," said Lil Mo.

"Bishkoko and Tilly are very special women," Martha Tom said. "They might seem strange to you, but not to Choctaws. They are bone pickers."

"They *were* human bones," whispered Lil Mo, "weren't they?"

"Yes," said Martha Tom. "An older man died, a few days after the Miracle Night. We did not say anything to your family about his death. You did not know him. You had other things to worry about."

"What happened to his body?" Lil Mo asked. "Why is he a skeleton?"

"A wagon carried his body down this path to a place in the woods not far from the bone pickers. When someone dies, the body lies outside till the flesh dries. Then the bone pickers remove the flesh and make a bone bundle. That's what she was doing, getting his body ready for burial."

"I remember Funi Man telling me something about bone bundles being buried in the woods, in small mounds," Lil Mo said. "But I didn't ask him where the bones came from."

"So now you know," said Martha Tom. "You should ask Funi Man to tell you more. I should not say anything else about it, not till Funi Man says it is all right."

"Yakoke," said Lil Mo. "I will."

The two walked for half a mile without speaking. Finally, Lil Mo asked, "Why were you there this morning?"

"The bone pickers never go to town," Martha Tom replied. "No one ever sees them but their closest friends. Someone has to bring them food and supplies. I was chosen by the council to be their helper."

"So you visit them often?"

"Yes. Now a question for you, Lil Mo," Martha Tom said. "Why were you at the house of the bone pickers?"

"I was chasing Ofijo. We got lost in the thunderstorm," said Lil Mo. Martha Tom said nothing. "And I was following some friends of mine."

"I think you have a secret, too," said Martha Tom. "Who are these friends?"

"I guess it's all right to tell you about them. Funi Man knows."

"They are Bohpoli, aren't they?" Martha Tom said. "You have Bohpoli friends, don't you? How many?"

"Four," said Lil Mo. "But I didn't see them this morning. I saw the green light. They carry a lantern, and sometimes I just see the light. I think they led me to the house of the bone pickers and left me there. On purpose."

"They are probably still laughing about you stumbling onto the house of bone pickers," Martha Tom said. "They love to play tricks, you know."

"I'm beginning to learn," Lil Mo replied. "But that's all right. They protect me, too."

"You were chosen, Lil Mo," she said. "Four is the most Bohpoli helpers I have ever heard of for one person. You could live your whole life and never know why they chose you."

"You were chosen, too," said Lil Mo. "You were chosen to take care of the bone pickers."

As they approached town, mud puddles lined the road, and the two stepped carefully. Martha Tom took Lil Mo's hand. They spoke not a word for the remainder of the walk, a walk that ended at Martha Tom's doorstep.

Lil Mo lifted his face and looked at Martha Tom. She returned his look.

"Chi pisa la chike," he said.

"Chi pisa la chike," said Martha Tom. "Till we meet again."

CHAPTER 31

Morning of Budding Romance

The next morning Martha Tom and her mother were cutting wild onions on the back porch. The sun was barely peeping over the pine trees, and the sky turned a brighter shade of blue with every passing minute. Red clouds streaked across the horizon.

"Maybe we can cook blackberry pudding for Lil Mo," Martha Tom said, talking as much to herself as to her mother. "Yes, I think maybe I should pick blackberries. Would that be hoke, Ma, if I pick blackberries this morning?"

Ella laughed out loud. She put down her slicing knife and looked at Martha Tom.

"What is it?" asked Martha Tom. "You don't think he would like blackberries?"

"Martha Tom, do you remember a time, several

months ago, when I asked you to pick blackberries?"

"How could I remember something that happened that long ago?" Martha Tom asked, rolling her eyes. Her mother laughed even harder.

"What is so funny?"

"Sweet little Martha Tom, you should remember!"

"Why?"

"Because you and those blackberries are the reason you met Lil Mo in the first place!" said Ella. "Here, take this basket. Stay on this side of the river, please, and go get Lil Mo his berries! We can cook the pudding as soon as you get back. Now go!"

"Yakoke," said Martha Tom, grabbing the basket and dashing across the fields to Lil Mo's new home. Then she remembered she was not going to see Lil Mo, not yet. She was going to the riverbank to pick blackberries. She laughed at her own silliness and turned to the river.

Hours later, rolling rain clouds covered the western sky. Martha Tom sat with Lil Mo under a low-drooping cottonwood tree in her backyard. They had just finished a meal of banaha bread and pashofa, thick and creamy corn chowder. Martha Tom was saving the blackberry pudding as a surprise.

"Lil Mo?"

"Yes, Martha Tom?" He always squirmed when she started off a conversation like this.

"What was it like, life on the other side?"

"Very different."

"I know that. But what did you do when you weren't working?"

"I worked all the time," Lil Mo said. They both knew he was lying just to irritate her.

"Hoke, if you don't want to talk about it, just sit like a log," she said.

"I can't sit like a log. Logs don't sit, they lie down."

"Were you like this before you met Funi Man?" Martha Tom asked. "Always trying to be funny?"

"It just came easy for me."

"Lil Mo, I am your friend, and I just want to know."

"Hoke," he said, smiling at how they teased each other. Joseph and Koi Losa, his other friends, were never like this. "I'll tell you what life was like on the plantation. We were afraid most of the time. We didn't think of ourselves as being afraid. If you asked any of the people who are still slaves right now if they are afraid, they would tell you no. They'd say they have family and friends. 'What is there to be afraid of?'

"But they would even be too afraid to answer. They'd be wondering, 'Who are you talking to? Will I get in trouble? Will anybody in my family get in trouble?' We were all the time afraid of getting in trouble."

"What happened when you got in trouble?"

Lil Mo did not reply.

"I'm asking what happened when you got in trouble, Lil Mo?"

"I did my best not to get in trouble," he replied.

"Except with Joseph," said Martha Tom. "You took a big risk for your friendship."

"Yes, but we are like brothers," Lil Mo said. "We've known each other from the time we were little kids."

"But tell me, Lil Mo, what happened if you got in trouble? Say somebody caught you playing with Joseph. What would they do to you?"

Lil Mo thought for a long time before speaking. He picked dried mud from the soles of his shoes. Martha Tom waited. She wrapped her arms around her knees and looked at Lil Mo.

"I was thinking about what happened to my mother," he finally said. "Bledsoe whipped my mother. Did I ever tell you that?"

"No, Lil Mo. I'm sorry I asked. I didn't mean to make you sad."

"Ahm achukma hoke," said Lil Mo.

"Ahm achukma hoke!" said Martha Tom, her eyes wide with wonder. "Lil Mo, you're learning Choctaw."

"Doesn't that mean 'I'm good, I'm all right'? Doesn't it?"

"Yes, it does. I am proud of you, Lil Mo." She kissed him on the cheek.

Lil Mo jumped to his feet. "Maybe I won't speak Choctaw anymore!"

"Lil Mo, don't be silly!"

"Me?" said Lil Mo. "Me don't be silly? I don't think I'm the silly one here!" He turned to go.

"What if I promise never to do that again?"

"That's not enough. You need to come up with something better than that."

"Hoke, Mr. Lil Mo," Martha Tom said in her singsong voice. "I was waiting for the right time to show you what I made today. Look at this!"

She lifted the bowl of blackberry pudding from the basket.

"Not worth it," said Lil Mo, without hesitating.

"Not worth what?"

"You promised, hoke?" he said.

"Lil Mo, I will not kiss you again if you beg me! Is that enough?"

"Hoke," said Lil Mo. "That and the blackberry pudding, that ought to be enough."

"I brought two spoons," Martha Tom said.

"Yakoke," said Lil Mo. Soon the black clay bowl, unable to withstand the two-spoon attack, sat empty between them.

"That was good," said Lil Mo, wiping pudding from his lips. "I should be going home. Plenty of work to do."

He turned to go, then stopped. He looked over his shoulder at Martha Tom.

"What is it?" she asked.

"Uh, do you need some help? Carrying everything in, washing things, anything? Hoke, never mind. I'm going. Hoke?"

"Lil Mo, I can carry the dishes to the house. I live here. My mother will help me wash them," she said, pointing to her house fifty feet away and trying to keep from laughing. Ella looked through a window and waved.

"I know that!" said Lil Mo. "Hoke. Chi pisa la chike."

"Chi pisa la chike, Lil Mo." Martha Tom watched Lil Mo disappear into the woods. She smiled and shook her head.

She had no way of knowing that she would never see *this* Lil Mo again, for Lil Mo would never be the same—after he met the owl man.

CHAPTER 32

Lil Mo and the Stranger

"Did he like the pudding?" asked Ella, as she and Martha Tom cleaned the dishes.

"Yes, he ate almost the whole bowl," said Martha Tom.

"Who was that man with him?"

"There was nobody with Lil Mo."

"I saw a man walking with him in the woods as he was leaving," her mother said. "I don't know the man. That's why I'm curious."

"I'll go see," Martha Tom said. She wiped her hands and hurried across the yard and into the woods. Lil Mo always took the same path home. He crossed the common cornfield, shared by everyone, then made his way west to his new house.

Martha Tom ran as quickly as she could. She soon spotted Lil Mo and an old man walking by his side on the banks of the river—far from his usual path. The man took small steps and stooped as he walked. The brim of his hat was pulled over his brow, covering his eyes.

"I know that man," she said to herself. She stopped and stared at him. Lil Mo was nodding his head and listening as the old man spoke. The man reached for Lil Mo, patting him on the shoulder.

"No!" Martha Tom said in a quiet whisper. She remembered how she knew the man.

She moved slowly behind a tree so they would not see her. Her mind flew to a time five years earlier. She was barely six years old. Her best friend at the time was a girl named Wilma. Wilma's father was not Choctaw. He looked Choctaw, but he was from another nation of people.

Martha Tom was too young to remember much about him. Wilma and her family moved away, to land her father's family owned. This was the first time she had ever lost a friend, and she remembered crying for days.

This man talking to Lil Mo was Wilma's uncle. He had come to Choctaw town to help with the move. But he only stayed a few days.

"Why did he leave?" Martha Tom asked herself. "Something happened." She looked again at the old man. He and Lil Mo were still talking, standing in the shadows of an old cottonwood tree. She crept close enough to hear what the old man was saying.

"Son, you are new here and you need to know how to protect yourself," the old man said. His voice was deep, and he spoke Choctaw very slowly. Martha Tom knew by his way of speaking that Choctaw was not his first language.

Lil Mo doesn't understand what he's saying, thought Martha Tom. *Lil Mo doesn't speak Choctaw!*

Lil Mo leaned close to the man, trying to understand.

The man soon realized Lil Mo didn't understand him. He began speaking English, and Lil Mo nodded and smiled.

Why did he leave? Mother would remember, Martha Tom thought. She almost turned for home, but something stopped her. The old man now held a small fan made of feathers. He waved it slowly as he spoke. Lil Mo reached for the feather fan.

"Keep these feathers with you all the time," the old man said. "If you don't trust someone, wait till after dark. Find yourself a place no one else knows about, maybe close to the river. I will teach you a song to protect yourself."

"No!" Martha Tom whispered to herself. She remembered more about the old man. As they were packing to move, Wilma's father had argued with a neighbor over a calf. The men had even had a fistfight, Martha Tom recalled. The old man appeared one night at the neighbor's house, and the next day the neighbor grew sick and almost died. The Choctaw council met and asked the old man to leave.

Finally, Martha Tom remembered.

The old man talking to Lil Mo is a witch, an owl witch! The Choctaw council knew he was a witch and made him leave.

The fan was made of owl feathers. She saw them now, five small owl feathers. Lil Mo held the fan as if it were a special gift. Martha Tom wanted to run, to let her parents know the owl witch had returned.

I can't leave Lil Mo with him, she thought.

Martha Tom heard a fluttering of leaves. Two large owls settled in a low-hanging branch of the cottonwood tree. They gripped the tree limb with large claws. One owl lifted and lowered his wings in a silent showing of power. The other raised a claw, flexing it like the fingers of a hand, and pointed the claw at Lil Mo. Three more owls flew to the tree and landed on higher limbs.

"You have enemies everywhere," the old man said, "more than you know. You have to watch and be very careful. People are saying things about you and your family. Bad things! You might think you are safe here, but you are not!"

"Everyone has been good to us," said Lil Mo. He looked confused. He heard the rustling in the leaves and looked above him. He saw the owls staring at him, as if awaiting an order. Dark clouds gathered, smelling of rain, and a cold breeze whistled.

"Think about that!" said the old man. "Everyone seems so kind and generous. There is no place on earth where everyone is good, no place! People will betray you, Lil Mo, you and your family both."

"Why would they hurt my family?" Lil Mo asked.

"A man or woman could get rich by selling your family," the old man said. "Slaves would bring a very high price, Lil Mo."

"How do you know my name?"

"I was sent to protect you. Trust me, I will be your protector."

The old man took the fan from Lil Mo. He looked to the tree limbs above and began to sing. His voice was soft, and he moved his feet in a standing dance as he wove his spell.

He waved the fan and chanted. The clouds grew darker, an owl hooted a sharp owl call, and soon several owls joined in the hooting. The old man chanted louder till his voice blended with the wind, the owl calls, the swaying of the trees.

He ducked his head and sang, but Lil Mo heard a whispering sound. The old man, though he danced and sang, still spoke to Lil Mo.

"Learn my song, Lil Mo. Sing my song and learn it.

When someone makes you angry, you must protect yourself. In secret, steal a strand of their hair. Wrap it around the handle of the fan. Sing the song and say their name. Sing it, Lil Mo!"

Martha Tom watched in horror as Lil Mo took the fan from the old man. He waved the fan and the owls screeched, louder than before. Lightning flashed, and Martha Tom covered her ears. A clap of thunder boomed and shook the tree.

Lil Mo stepped in time with the old man and rain began to fall. Hard raindrops pelted the two, the owl man and Lil Mo, but still they danced. Martha Tom shook her head. She screamed "Stop!", but her voice was unheard.

The old man lifted his hand slowly to Lil Mo, so slowly Lil Mo saw only the driving rain, only the wind-driven leaves swirling around his face. His eyes drooped, and he mumbled the words to the old man's song. Lil Mo was lost to the world of Choctaw town and Bok Chitto. He swooned, unseeing, in a world of darkness.

Lil Mo never felt it when the witch man took a tuft of his hair. The old man gripped Lil Mo's hair between his bony fingers and plucked it from his head. He rolled the hair into a tiny ball and tucked it into a leather bag hanging from his belt.

Martha Tom saw everything. She fell to her knees, unable to move. Her mouth dropped open as she tried to speak. No words came. She shivered and shook, partly from the cold and partly at the sight before her.

Lil Mo stood helpless beneath the witch man's spell.

"Your enemies are coming, Lil Mo," the witch man whispered. "Hide the fan and never let them know you have it."

Lil Mo tucked the fan under his shirt. His skin burned at the touch of the owl feathers. Blisters rose on his belly. He flung himself into the dance, waving his arms and stepping faster.

CHAPTER 33

Seeds of Doubt

"Where is Martha Tom?" Ella asked herself.

She watched the clouds gathering. Unlike the usual clouds that rose slowly over the horizon, these clouds appeared suddenly, with no warning.

"These clouds are a sign of trouble," she said aloud.

They hovered over a single spot, close to the river. With a sudden flash of memory, Ella recalled the old man she had seen walking with Lil Mo. She hurried to the cornfield.

"Funi Man, help! I need you!" she shouted as she neared the workers. Funi Man, Lavester, and several other men joined her at the edge of the field.

"Lil Mo is with an old man, a witch man that was here before!" she said. "Funi Man, you remember him. The council made him leave."

"I do remember him," said Funi Man, "and he is evil. He should never be talking to Lil Mo!"

"Martha Tom followed them to the river. She must still be there."

"We should hurry," Funi Man called over his shoulder to his followers. He carried his shotgun on his hip as he ran. Koi Losa rushed to join them.

"You can go with us," Funi Man cautioned him, "but stay behind the others. Lil Mo is with a witch. You must not try anything to save him. Let the elders do their work."

Koi Losa nodded. He gripped his fist and hot tears filled his eyes. His friend was in danger and he could do nothing to help.

The Choctaws saw the gathering clouds and knew that serious danger was approaching. As they neared the river, a bolt of lightning struck a cedar tree. It burst into flames before them. Like the skin of an open wound, the sky split apart, and rainwater drenched the rescue party.

Led by Funi Man, they circled the tree and hurried to the center of the storm. Funi Man held his hand up when they reached the cottonwood tree. They watched as the old man sang and danced in the downpour. Lil Mo moved his feet as well, staring at the old man with a far-away look in his eyes.

Martha Tom's mother pointed overhead, and all eyes

turned to see the owls, now numbering several dozen. Unfazed by the lightning and pounding rain, they gripped the tree limbs. They lifted their wings and raised their claws in a slow and eerie dance without rhythm.

Funi Man brought his shotgun to his shoulder, aiming at the witch. The owl man lifted his face to the sky and screeched a cry so loud it stung everyone's eardrums. He shook his arms over his head and moved his feet in a circle. Faster and faster he spun, till he vanished in a whirling blur of motion.

Funi Man fired his gun. A puff of smoke rose from the barrel. Buckshot struck the trunk of the cottonwood, and bits of tree bark floated to the ground. The old man stopped spinning, and before them stood an owl, the largest owl they had ever seen.

His square head was covered with brown-and-gray feathers. The owl blinked his yellow eyes and swiveled his head. Everyone watched as he slowly raised his long, wide wings. With one downward thrust of his wings, he soared above the treetops. Lil Mo fell to the ground.

The owl man hovered for a brief moment, then circled the tree. With a rustling of leaves, the other owls flew away to join him.

Funi Man dropped his gun and ran to Lil Mo.

"Wake up, Lil Mo!" he said. "We are here for you, son."

"Where is Martha Tom?" asked her mother.

Lil Mo sat up and looked at the growing crowd. His chest heaved, and he seemed lost to all understanding.

"I know she is here somewhere," said Ella. "Martha Tom followed him. I didn't remember who the witch owl was till she was already gone!"

Lavester knelt at Lil Mo's side. "Son," he said, "if you can help us, please do. Do you remember seeing Martha Tom?"

"Please, Lil Mo," asked Ella, "where is she?"

Hidden by a clump of bushes, Martha Tom sat shivering on the wet ground. She heard her mother call her name, but still she sat. Her teeth chattered, and she could not make them stop. She was more cold and afraid than she had ever been in her life. Wet brown leaves fell from a branch above her. They dropped in her hair and on her face. She never even noticed.

"Mother," she said, so soft and trembling that no one heard. "Mother," she said, over and over, wrapping her arms around herself. She closed her eyes and whispered, "I am afraid for everyone." Her mind wandered, and she dreamed.

CHAPTER 34

Who Is This Lil Mo?

Martha Tom woke up to see everyone gathered around Lil Mo. She yawned, stood up, and stretched her arms. "I am soaked," she said. "My clothes are wet." No one noticed her. They all stared at Lil Mo.

"Where is she?" Funi Man asked again.

Martha Tom joined the circle of people surrounding Lil Mo. She elbowed her way through the crowd and whispered to a young man she barely knew. "Who are they looking for?"

"Martha Tom," he answered, without looking at her.

"Oh," said Martha Tom. "Is she in trouble?"

"We think so," the man replied.

"Well," said Martha Tom, "I'll let you know if I see her. I better be going now."

"Yes," said the man. "You shouldn't be here. Run along home now."

"I will," said Martha Tom. "Maybe by the time they find me, they won't be mad anymore," she said as she tiptoed quietly away.

"There she is!" yelled Funi Man.

Martha Tom slipped on the muddy ground, her dream-spell broken. "Whatever it is, I didn't do it!" she hollered.

In the strong arms of her mother, Martha Tom was carried home—far from the witch owl, far from the dark and evil dance. Lil Mo followed, carried by his Choctaw uncle, Funi Man.

With the witch gone, the sunlight returned, peeping through the red-streaked clouds. Slick mud sparkled on the riverbank and frogs began to croak. Birds of the more normal sort—mockingbirds, cardinals, and sparrows— shook their wings dry and hopped from limb to limb in search of insects.

Soon everyone gathered by the fire in Martha Tom's house. Choctaw men guarded the building at front and back. Inside, everyone sipped pashofa and waited for the story. Surrounded by Lil Mo's family, Martha Tom spoke first.

She spoke of the owls flocking to the tree. She told of the swirling winds, and the clouds that came as if they were called, as if they were alive. She told of Lil Mo's innocence, his belief that the witch spoke the truth. She told of the dance of the owl man, the chanting, and of

Lil Mo finally giving himself over to the spell.

But she said nothing of the fan—the fan of owl feathers that Lil Mo carried still lay tucked beneath his shirt.

Lil Mo listened, limp from exhaustion. The flickering light from the fire colored his cheeks yellow and red. As the story unfolded, Martha Tom's voice rose. Her urgent hands sent shadows around the room. As she invoked the fear she felt, the listeners gazed at Lil Mo. His face showed no expression.

Martha Tom finished by telling of passing out, then coming to her senses slowly as everyone appeared. When her story was over, everyone waited for Lil Mo to tell of his experience.

"I am too tired to talk," he said. "I will be better tomorrow."

Well past midnight, the gathering broke up.

"I think Lil Mo should stay with us tonight," said Ella. "Why don't you stay as well?" she asked, turning to Treda and Lavester.

"Yakoke," said Treda, "but we should be home. I want to take Angel home, where she can feel safe."

"I will stay here and look out for Lil Mo," Funi Man said.

"Thank you," Treda said as she held Lil Mo close. "I will come for breakfast," she whispered to him. "Sleep well."

"Good night, son," Lavester said. "You are stronger than this. Remember who you are."

Funi Man rolled out his blanket by the fire, next to Lil Mo.

"We can talk in the morning," said Funi Man. "I'll wake you up early. I am right next to you if you need me during the night."

Lil Mo stared at the red-hot coals for only a minute before his eyelids closed. "Funi Man," he mumbled, half asleep.

"Yes?"

"I left Ofijo home today. I am glad I did."

"Me too," said Funi Man. "That old man would not like Ofijo."

"Would he have hurt Ofijo?" Lil Mo asked.

"Maybe we would be feasting on owl wings tonight if Ofijo had been there."

"That's what I thought," said Lil Mo. "He would have killed him, wouldn't he?"

"Go to sleep, Lil Mo, and be thankful you didn't bring Ofijo."

Lil Mo rolled into his blanket.

"Lil Mo?" said Funi Man.

"What?"

"Why didn't you bring Ofijo?"

"I was having lunch with Martha Tom," Lil Mo said.

"She makes such a fuss about Ofijo. She says he is the most handsome thing she's ever seen. I just wanted to eat and go home."

Funi Man did not reply.

"Whatever you're thinking," said Lil Mo, "It's not funny!"

"Go to sleep," said Funi Man.

"You too," said Lil Mo.

The witch owl man had achieved his purpose. He had planted seeds of mistrust. By evening time the next day, every Choctaw family spoke quietly to their children. They warned them once more of owls and the evil they sometimes carried. And now a new name was mentioned in connection with the owls.

"The new young man who lives among us, Lil Mo. He was seen today, dancing with the owls." That was how the mothers warned their children. That was what uncles told their nephews.

Funi Man and Ella heard the rumors.

"We have healing to do," they said. "We put our faith in healing."

CHAPTER 35

Bad Dreams

Lil Mo called out during the night, but only once. When Funi Man touched his shoulder, he jerked away.

"No!" he yelled.

"Chim achukma?" asked Funi Man, asking how Lil Mo felt.

"Ahm achukma hoke, yakoke," Lil Mo replied. "I am good, thank you." He rolled closer to the fire and closed his eyes tight. As he shifted his weight, the feather fan rubbed against an open blister. Lil Mo grimaced. He knew Funi Man was watching him, so he lay still and breathed easily.

Funi Man will think I am asleep, he thought.

"Is everything all right?" Ella asked, stepping out of her bedroom. "I thought I heard Lil Mo."

"Yes," said Funi Man. "He had a bad dream."

She pulled up a chair by the fire and wrapped a shawl over her shoulders. "Did you wake him up?"

"I asked him if he was hoke. He seems to be. He fell back to sleep easy enough."

"Has he talked to you yet about what happened?"

"No, we'll do that tomorrow."

"Somebody needs to keep an eye on his family, too," she said. "Treda is more worried than I have ever seen her."

Lil Mo listened closely to everything that was said. *"Somebody needs to keep an eye on his family"!* he thought. *Why would she say that? Why does somebody need to watch my family? Maybe she is afraid my family will escape, like before.*

Lil Mo heard the song, softly at first. He heard the old man singing. His muscles twitched, and he felt himself moving to the song. The owl feathers were warm on his belly. He touched the fan.

Suddenly, Lil Mo was on the roof of the house. He stood tall and stretched his arms to the sky, the dark night sky. A full moon beamed, outshining the stars. Lil Mo felt strong, as if he could fly, and he realized he was not alone.

He looked to his feet and saw first one owl, then another, then still another, till he was surrounded by twenty owls, maybe more. Some were brown winged, like those in the cottonwood tree. Others were solid white with thick feathers.

A large white owl flew in a circle around Lil Mo's head.

His feet stomped out the rhythm of the old man's song as he turned 'round and 'round on the rooftop. His mind filled with a memory of Harold and a large white owl.

Barn owls, he thought. *Harold shot a barn owl one day, I remember. The owl fell from the rafters to the ground and flapped his wings till he died.*

"You killed it!" Lil Mo cried out. "You shot the barn owl!"

"Lil Mo, wake up!" Funi Man pulled the blanket from Lil Mo and held him by the shoulders. "You're in Martha Tom's house, and we are here for you!"

Lil Mo shook from head to toe.

"Hoke, Lil Mo. Everything is hoke," said Funi Man.

Lil Mo lifted his head and gazed around the darkened room. Funi Man knelt by his side. Ella stood over him with Martha Tom clinging to her skirt.

"I am sorry," Lil Mo said. "I didn't mean to wake you up."

"Don't worry about that," Ella said. "Just know that you are here with people who care for you."

Lil Mo nodded, but another voice crept into the room, heard only by him. "Everyone seems so kind and generous!" said the voice. "Do you see, Lil Mo? Just like I warned you! People will betray you, Lil Mo, you and your family both."

"No!" Lil Mo cried, shaking his head. "I don't believe you!"

"Lil Mo," said Funi Man. "It's me, Funi Man. Look at me, Lil Mo. You are in Martha Tom's house."

Lil Mo covered his face with his hands. "I know where I am. Please, can I go back to sleep?"

The next morning at breakfast, Lil Mo sat with Funi Man, Ella, and Martha Tom. Soft rain fell, dripping sweet music from the porch roof as the other three chatted. Lil Mo took his bowl and nodded a silent yakoke. He listened to the words *behind* everything that was spoken. Mostly, he listened to the voice that sang.

The old man's chanting grew so loud in his head he looked up to see if anyone else heard it. He set his food aside and stepped out to the porch. Through the window he saw people leaning close, speaking quietly to each other.

"Quietly, so I won't hear them," he heard himself saying. "Now that I'm gone they're talking. Now that I cannot hear them."

"The witch made his mark on Lil Mo," Funi Man said. "I will keep him with me today. Will you let Treda know when she comes?"

"Of course. Should we let Shonti know?" Ella asked.

"Yes," said Funi Man. "She can help."

"If I know Shonti, she already knows more than we do about what happened," Ella said.

Lil Mo looked over his shoulder at Ella and Funi Man.

They passed the serving bowl back and forth and spoke in low voices. He knew they were his friends. But the old man's voice grew stronger.

"Everyone seems so kind and generous!" he heard the old man say. Lil Mo stepped from the porch and turned to the river.

"I have only one friend," he said to himself, "Joseph. I don't need their help to cross the river. I am old enough. I can swim."

He walked faster, and when he saw Funi Man step through the door to follow him, he broke into a run. He crossed the field and made his way to the cottonwood tree. Looking over his shoulder, he saw Funi Man running after him.

Lil Mo slapped the tree trunk, and the leaves above him shivered. Raindrops fell from thick yellow leaves. Lil Mo lifted his face to the wet drops. Through the leaves above him, he saw a thick white ball of feathers. The barn owl.

As Lil Mo watched, the owl shook his feathers, and more wet drops fell on his face. These drops were thick and red. He ran his hands across his cheeks and spread the red drops on his face. Blood of the snow owl spotted his brow and chin and rolled across his lips.

The old man appeared again and smiled at Lil Mo. The man had feathers sprouting from his sleeves. He dipped his head and began to dance, a slow, stomping dance. Lil Mo joined in as the man made his way to the river.

"Your friends are there," the old man said. "Go to your friends."

Lil Mo closed his eyes and followed the sound of the stomping, the chanting of the owl man. The mud was thick, but Lil Mo's feet lifted and stomped through bushes and vines. The owl man's call was strong.

Cold fingers gripped Lil Mo's feet, cold, wet fingers. He danced faster, to drive away the chill, but the feeling crept higher, from his legs to his waist. He waved his arms to the chanting. His legs were heavy, and Lil Mo could barely move them.

"Lil Mo!"

Lil Mo heard the call, but the sound of chanting was stronger. He opened his eyes and saw the owl man, now covered with feathers, reaching for him. Lil Mo was standing in the river Bok Chitto, chest deep in the cold water. Still he walked, and the water rose to claim him.

"Lil Mo!" The sound of his name flew like a warm breeze from the Choctaw shore. "Lil Mo!" He turned and saw Funi Man. The fog grew thick, and Funi Man disappeared.

In slow motion, Lil Mo danced. His head was underwater, but his feet moved to the chanting. New friends called to him. Not with words or chanting, but with open arms they called. They swam like fish. Their bodies were covered with scales, but they swam with arms and legs as people swim.

White as the barn owl, they came for him. Slick, cold arms wrapped around Lil Mo. *A new home*, he thought. *They will take me to their home.*

"Go with them," said the owl man. The fish people gripped Lil Mo tight and pulled him to the river bottom.

CHAPTER 36

Lil Mo and the Fish People

"Lil Mo! It's me, Funi Man. I'm here for you!"

For the first time, the water felt cold, bitterly cold. The chanting ceased, the spell was broken, and Lil Mo saw the fish people, the Owa Naholo.

White as death, their eyes were large and had no eyelids. Their mouths were blue and pink, and fish gills puffed and blew where cheeks should be. Their grip was mean, and their fingers clung to him like claws.

Lil Mo wrestled his arms free and thrust his hands through the surface of the water. The fish people clung to his legs, but Funi Man was stronger. He gripped Lil Mo by the wrists and slowly pulled him free, leaving the fish people swimming inches from the surface.

Funi Man would never forget how the Owa Naholo looked at him as he lifted Lil Mo from their grasp. Their mouths opened and closed, as if they longed to speak. Their big eyes pleaded with him to save them, too, to carry them far away from this cold river. But their arms were ready to grab him, should he step close to the water.

"You don't want to be saved," he said to the fish people. "You only want more victims." He carried Lil Mo to the base of a sycamore tree and laid him on the leafy forest floor.

Lil Mo curled into a small round ball. Funi Man leaned against the tree trunk and ran his fingers through his hair, watching sun rays dance across the water.

"Yakoke, Holitopama. Yakoke," he whispered, raising his face to the morning sky. He stooped to Lil Mo and patted the back of his head.

As the fog lifted, Funi Man carried his sleeping friend far from the river bottom, the home of the Owa Naholo. He carried him to his own home, nestled in the cornfields of Choctaw town.

Funi Man built a cedar fire, and soon the sweet smoke filled his house. With Lil Mo safely tucked in a pile of blankets by the fire, Funi Man moved to the porch. He settled on a chair and looked to the cornfield and the piney woods beyond. From a leather pouch he took two foot-long sticks, his chant sticks. He closed his eyes and began to sing, snapping out a rhythm with the sticks.

Lil Mo opened his eyes. Seeing he was nestled in a corner of Funi Man's home, he closed his eyes and fell into the music. An owl called, but his song was muted by the morning. A young robin shot across the sky. A mockingbird joined the singing, and Lil Mo knew he was safe in the cedar smoke and Choctaw song of Funi Man.

An hour later, Lil Mo sat up and wrapped the blanket over his shoulders.

"Funi Man," he said, rubbing his eyes. He felt the sting of the owl feather fan against his stomach. The pain of the blister wouldn't go away. "Are you awake yet? I am ready to talk."

"I never went to sleep," said Funi Man, stepping in from the porch. "Let me get some water boiling." Lil Mo sat silent as Funi Man made two cups of sassafras root tea.

The cup felt warm in Lil Mo's palms. He wondered where to begin. He blew the tea to cool it, sipped once, and set the cup aside. Funi Man waited without looking at Lil Mo.

"I never saw the man before," Lil Mo said. "But there are lots of people in Choctaw town I have never seen. I wasn't worried. He didn't talk or dress like everybody else. I should have asked him where he came from."

"Son, you cannot blame yourself for anything that happened."

"Hoke," said Lil Mo. "I wish it was that easy, this not blaming yourself."

Funi Man nodded and smiled. "You are growing up before my eyes," he said. "I am very proud of you."

"Yakoke. I am glad you are my uncle. My father and mother would never know what to think about the old man."

"They haven't lived here, Lil Mo. They can't know everything on both sides of the river."

"I know. I am sorry." Lil Mo sipped his tea. "You are really good at waiting," he said. Funi Man shrugged and took a sip of his own tea. "You're not going to ask me anything?"

Funi Man shook his head. "Not yet," he said. "You're doing fine."

"I don't want to believe what he told me," Lil Mo continued. "He said people here, Choctaw people, would try to sell us. We would be slaves again. He said I could not trust anyone. When I asked him why, he said for the money."

"Witches are the best at spreading lies," Funi Man said. "They use this gossip to come between friends." He paused and felt the next question linger on his lips before he spoke it. "Lil Mo, do you trust me?"

"Yes. I trust you more than anybody."

Funi Man said nothing. He knew Lil Mo had a secret,

one he didn't want to think about or tell.

The feather fan poked against Lil Mo's stomach. The feathers were cold and wet from the blood of the popped blister.

"Will you not blame me?" Lil Mo asked, turning away from Funi Man.

"Lil Mo, after what you and your family have gone through, how could anyone blame you?"

"Hoke," said Lil Mo. He lifted his shirt and pulled out the feather fan. He winced at the pain of the wooden handle against his tender skin.

Funi Man felt his heart beat faster. He saw the owl feathers, shiny and wet with Lil Mo's blood. He wanted to grab the fan and fling it out the door. Instead, he sipped his tea and waited.

Lil Mo laid the fan on the floor and looked at Funi Man.

"The man gave me this. He told me never to tell anyone I had it."

"Did he say what to do with it?"

"Not at first," said Lil Mo. "But I saw him dance and wave the fan, looking at me. Funi Man, his eyes grew big, like a deep yellow hole. I felt myself falling in. He taught me how to sing and wave the fan."

"What else did he tell you? Can you remember?"

"I remember he talked about what to do if anybody made me mad. He said to pick some of their hair and wrap it around the handle of the fan while I sang. Bad things would happen to them, that's what he said."

Lil Mo pulled his knees up close and wrapped his arms around them. He rocked back and forth. "I am afraid," he finally said.

"You are right to be afraid," said Funi Man. "The man was trying to turn you, son, to make you like him. He is full of hatred. He wants to punish anyone who crosses him."

"No forgiving. That is his road, isn't it?"

"That's right, Lil Mo. He takes the road of no forgiving. It is a lonely and dark road."

"Can you help me?"

"Yes, Lil Mo. I will do everything I can for you," Funi Man said, sipping his tea. "But Shonti knows more than I do about healing. I'll take you to her."

"Did I hear my name?"

Lil Mo smiled for the first time in a day. He looked at Funi Man, who shrugged his shoulders and laughed. Shonti stood at the door.

Lil Mo looked at her feet. *I wonder if she brought her friends, the ones that crawl and rattle?* he thought.

Not a good idea, Funi Man thought back, so Lil Mo said nothing. He gathered the blanket around his shoulders and waited for whatever magic Shonti brought.

CHAPTER 37

Snakes of Shonti

"Come in," said Funi Man. "We are already awake."

"Achukma," Shonti said. "Funi Man, I want you to stay close."

"Lil Mo, hide the fan. She will take it from you," the old man hissed, unheard by the others.

Lil Mo shook his head.

"Guard the fan. It is your only hope to save your family."

"My family." Lil Mo moved his lips in reply. "My family, yes. I must protect my family!"

He fought to stop his hand as it crept across the floor, but he could not. While Funi Man stood to welcome Shonti, he clutched the fan and quickly tucked it to his belly.

Funi Man pulled a chair by the fire for Shonti and

stepped to the corner of the room, waiting. Shonti sat by Lil Mo and unfurled a dark red cloth. She took a single feather from the cloth and laid it on her lap.

Lil Mo's eyes grew large, and he looked to Funi Man. The feather was soft tan and white. "Is that . . . ?"

Shonti held up her hand for silence. "Yes, it is an owl feather. A single feather can protect you. No talking now."

Lil Mo wanted to tell her about the feathers now twitching on his belly. *She already knows*, he thought. The feathers grew warm, and his skin itched. The blisters burned, and he gritted his teeth to keep from crying out in pain.

"Lil Mo, are you hoke?" asked Funi Man.

Lil Mo nodded, but tears welled up in his eyes and streamed down his cheeks. He nodded faster, and his whole body rocked and shook. He leaned toward Funi Man with his mouth stretched wide open.

"Leave me alone!" Lil Mo shouted in a cracked and hissing voice. He flung his head back and spit across the room at Funi Man. "Go away and leave Lil Mo alone. You only want the money for yourself!"

Lil Mo heard these words come from his mouth, in the owl man's voice. He shook his head with a violence he had never known. He tried to tell Funi Man it was not he who spoke, but no words came out. The muscles of his neck flexed and froze. Lil Mo could no longer control what he did or said.

"This will happen," said Shonti to Funi Man. "The witch is strong and will have his say. This is not Lil Mo, you must know that."

Funi Man took his chant sticks from his pocket. He pressed his back against the wall and slid slowly down to sit upon the floor. He leaned forward and tapped the sticks together, and Shonti nodded her approval.

Like small, quick worms they came, darting to every crack and corner of the room. In an instant they grew and became the rattlesnakes. The room shivered with their whirring. From the ceiling they dangled. From cracks in the floor, from walls and windows, from every place they hung and twisted. Their flicking tongues danced like flames. The snakes of Shonti curled around the house.

Though the words flew from his own mouth, Lil Mo felt like a spectator. He could only watch and listen as the owl man's voice grew louder and louder.

"They are not your people, Lil Mo! Look at them. Look at yourself. Why would they help you?"

Lil Mo closed his eyes and moved his fingers to his mouth. He felt his lips moving, saying the words, and hoped no one else could hear. He opened his eyes and saw a strange and hurtful look on Funi Man's face.

"You hear me, don't you," the owl witch said. "Yes,

both of you hear me, and you know I tell the truth. Leave this boy alone!"

"Lil Mo, if you can understand me, you are safe," said Funi Man. "You are still with us. Stay strong and know that we are here for you. Always, Lil Mo."

Lil Mo felt a burning on his scalp. His hand moved to the spot where the owl man had taken his hair.

"What is it?" asked Funi Man.

"The witch took a piece of his hair," Shonti said. "He's using it to get to Lil Mo. As long as he is alive, Lil Mo is in serious danger."

"Lies! Lies!" the voice hissed. "Listen to their lies and you die a slave, Lil Mo. I have come to free you!"

The room disappeared, and Lil Mo stood in the darkest of nights, in a wet and swampy clearing in the woods. Slimy green water covered most of the ground. An ancient cypress tree loomed over him, and moss sagged from the branches, surrounding him like a spiderweb.

There is no escape from this place, Lil Mo thought.

"Yes, Lil Mo," the voice said. "Nothing but death will walk away from here."

Funi Man and Shonti watched as Lil Mo curled into a ball on the floor. "What is happening?" Funi Man asked.

"Lil Mo is in a dream world," Shonti said. "I will take care of him as best I can. You must take care of the witch, Funi Man, if we ever want to see Lil Mo again. I will let his parents know why I must keep him here."

Funi Man gathered his shotgun and ammunition. He packed his saddlebag with two shirts, a bundle of dried pork, and bark for tea, then quickly made his way to the barn behind his house. He saddled his horse, Hawkeye, patting him gently and stroking his ears.

"Looks like we'll be going on a trip," he said softly. Hawkeye stomped and nodded, as if he understood. Funi Man tossed six pelts of fox fur on Hawkeye's hindquarters. As he led him through the barn door, Funi Man spotted something leaning in a dusty corner.

"I have not used you in years and years," he said aloud. "The shotgun didn't work on the owl before. Maybe it's time for some old Choctaw hunting."

He picked up the blow-dart gun, a hollowed-out piece of seven-foot river cane, and six darts made of sharp thorns and twigs.

"Yakoke, Grandpa," he said. "I promise to take better care of your gift. Yakoke."

Funi Man stood at the door and watched the dark clouds gathering. He remembered the day his grandfather had given him the blow-dart gun. "I was the same age as Koi Losa, a little older than Lil Mo is now," he said to himself. "I was quite a shot to be so young!"

He returned to the barn and saddled a second pony. Shonti stood on the porch, waiting for him to pass. "You will need some powerful poison," she said. "I gathered some plants for you last night." She tossed him a cloth bundle.

Funi Man replied with a tight smile. "What would we do without you, Shonti?"

"Ilvppa ittibai foyuka, Funi Man," she said, returning to Lil Mo. She was right, Funi Man knew—they were all in this together.

CHAPTER 38

Witch Hunters

Koi Losa stood up from his bed of leaves. He yawned and stretched, keeping a sharp eye on Funi Man's house. Soon after sunrise he heard Lil Mo call out in the voice of the owl man. He crept closer and peered through a small window. Whirring sounds came from the log walls.

No one could enter that house now, not with Shonti and her rattlesnakes guarding it, he thought, backing away.

Koi Losa watched as Funi Man led his pony from the barn, saddled and ready to ride. He saw Funi Man pause.

He is thinking about me, Koi Losa thought. *"Maybe Koi Losa would be handy to have around," that's what he's thinking.*

Funi Man turned to the barn and soon appeared with the second pony.

"Yes!" Koi Losa shouted. He stepped from the trees.

"What are you doing?" Funi Man asked.

"Waiting for you, Funi Man," Koi Losa said.

"I've been inside waiting for you!"

"I think you are trying to be funny," said Koi Losa.

"You are getting more like Lil Mo everyday."

"I hope so," said Koi Losa.

The two witch hunters, Funi Man and Koi Losa, smiled at each other. They knew their playful words hid the nature of their journey. Lil Mo's life was in danger, and the danger was darker than Bledsoe and his whip, more powerful than anything they had ever faced.

"Ilvppa ittibai foyuka," Funi Man said. "We are all in this together."

They rode side by side on the road going north from Choctaw town. As they passed friends on the road, Funi Man spoke and waved, but didn't stop to visit.

"Is it a good idea that everybody sees us?" asked Koi Losa. "What if the witch finds out he is being tracked?"

"Koi Losa, the witch has too many owl friends to hide anything from him. They fly overhead. They hide in the trees. They watch from far away and so close they can feel you breathing. Day and night, at every moment."

Koi Losa looked to the sky and the treetops.

"You won't see them," said Funi Man. "Not unless they want to be seen."

"But why do we want him to know we are after him?"

"If he knows we are after him, he may come for us

sooner. That is what I want. I am too old to chase a witch for hundreds of miles."

Koi Losa said nothing, and they rode in silence for most of the morning. Koi Losa kept a keen eye on the tree limbs above them, while Funi Man kept his head low and listened.

By early afternoon, they reached the outskirts of Scottville, a nahullo town surrounded by small farms and one large plantation. They halted in front of a store with a wooden sign above the window that read TEMPLE'S TRADING POST.

The front door stood wide open and Koi Losa saw Choctaw and Chickasaw men and women crowding around a counter. Koi Losa and Funi Man dismounted, tied their ponies to a porch rail, and stepped inside the store.

A stout nahullo man stood behind the counter.

"Who's next?" he called out.

"Mr. Temple, I think it was this gentleman," said his helper. He pointed to a leather-faced old Choctaw man with a clay pot under each arm.

"Thank you, Martin," Mr. Temple said. "Okay, let's take a look at those pots." The old man placed the pots on the counter and kept his eyes on the floor.

Martin moved in a quick, nervous way. His arms and legs were thin as broomsticks, and everything about him was spiffy clean. He peered at the pots through round spectacles, which kept slipping down the bridge of his nose.

When he finished looking at the pots, Martin scribbled something in a book and showed it to Temple.

"Thank you, Martin," Mr. Temple said.

"Watch closely, Koi Losa," Funi Man said. "This is where iskuli comes from. The nahullos call it money."

Koi Losa nodded and stepped closer to the counter. He wanted to see what money looked like. The witch owl claimed Lil Mo's friends only wanted money.

What thing could be so beautiful that people would betray their friends for it? he asked himself. He watched as Mr. Temple handed two small pieces of paper to the Choctaw man.

"Who's next?" Mr. Temple said. The man stuffed the paper in his pants pocket. He took a long, deep breath, gave a last look at the pots, and turned to the door.

"Where is the iskuli?" Koi Losa asked.

"The paper," said Funi Man. "That was the money."

"The Choctaw elder traded his pots for two pieces of paper? That is money?"

"That is money," Funi Man said. "That is what so many people die for."

Koi Losa dropped his jaw and stared at Funi Man. He knew he would never understand. He didn't want to understand. He watched as one by one the Choctaws and

211

Chickasaws traded their belongings for pieces of paper money—iskuli.

"We need money, too," said Funi Man. "When you leave Choctaw town and you want to eat, you need iskuli."

"We can hunt and eat what we catch," Koi Losa said.

"Not in nahullo country. You can't kill a deer or catch a fish. You might be on someone else's land. Just watch, Koi Losa. This will be a good learning day for you. Now, bring me the fox pelts."

Koi Losa hurried to Funi Man's pony and returned with the red fox pelts. Funi Man was next in line. He dropped the pelts on the counter.

Martin counted the skins and wrote numbers in the book. "Six fox skins," he said to Mr. Temple. Mr. Temple handed Funi Man two pieces of paper.

"Yakoke," he said, tipping his hat and pocketing the money.

As they climbed onto their ponies, Koi Losa asked, "Why does that Mr. Temple have all the money, anyway? Where did he get it?"

"Good question," Funi Man said. "I don't know where he got it."

"He was in a hurry."

"Iskuli does that to people, Koi Losa. They want to hurry more than they want to spend time with other people. They like money more."

"More than people? They like money more than people?"

Funi Man nodded. "Yes. More than people."

"Funi Man, no one could like pieces of paper more than people!" Koi Losa said, laughing.

"Mr. Temple and Martin, they both do. You need to know this, Koi Losa. Everything changes with iskuli."

Koi Losa rode for a moment without speaking. He wished Lil Mo were here. *He would know what to say about iskuli,* Koi Losa thought. *Lil Mo is better at talking than I am.* He smiled as he thought of Lil Mo.

As they rode away from the trading post, Funi Man headed toward the forest on the edge of town. He pulled Hawkeye off the road and into the trees.

Koi Losa followed. "Where are we going?" he asked.

Funi Man said nothing as a dangerous thought crossed his mind. The world went suddenly dark, and a vision emerged.

Funi Man saw Lil Mo, curled up in the corner of his house. Shonti stood over him. She passed a burning bundle of cedar over Lil Mo's head, circling the room, smoking the house with the sweet and cleansing smell of cedar. In the trees surrounding the house, in the dark shadows of leaves, the owls were gathering.

In Funi Man's vision, Lil Mo slipped up behind Shonti. He grabbed the cedar bundle and threw it on Funi Man's bed. The blankets caught fire, and Lil Mo wrestled Shonti to the ground. The entire house burst into flames. All Funi Man could see was a cloud of dark smoke rising.

Out from the clouds of smoke flew owls of every size and color. They swirled and dipped and soared through the cloud of darting, hungry flames.

"No!" Funi Man called out.

"Funi Man," Koi Losa said, tugging Funi Man's shirt. "You sound like Lil Mo. Are you hoke?"

"Yes," Funi Man said. "The owl is nearby, Koi Losa. He took my thoughts and gave me dark ones."

CHAPTER 39

Whisper and Wait

Funi Man and Koi Losa rode deeper into the woods, following a path through the trees. They rode without speaking for almost an hour.

"Whoa!" Funi Man hollered, as the path ended and they burst through the trees. He jerked on the reins and held out his hand to stop Koi Losa. Before them loomed a limestone cliff, a sharp drop-off to a creek bed a hundred feet below.

Koi Losa toppled forward as his pony came to a quick halt. The pony stamped his front hooves and skidded, sending rocks tumbling down the face of the cliff.

"Guess this tells us why nobody has farmed this land," Funi Man said. "Too dangerous. Looks like a good place to camp for the night."

"Are you sure?" Koi Losa asked.

"Can you think of any place the witch would rather find us than here, next to a cliff?"

"No, I can't," said Koi Losa. He climbed off his pony and leaned over the edge. "A long way to fall," he added, seeing the thin trickle of water below.

"I am too old to be away from home," said Funi Man. "I want this over with."

Koi Losa started to say something, but he caught the words before they could be heard. *I don't want to go home dead*, he thought instead.

"Don't be afraid, Koi Losa. It's a long way for the owl to fall, too. We just have to make sure he's falling with broken wings."

"Funi Man," Koi Losa said, shaking his head, "you would be funny in the face of death."

"Where do you think we are?" asked Funi Man. "You will never be as close to death as you are right now, two feet from this cliff with that peering down at you." He pointed to the outstretched limb of a pine tree.

Koi Losa looked up and saw a white barn owl lift his wings in warning. His wingspan was so big it blocked the sun, but only for a moment. A dark shadow, borne of the owl, inched across the ground. It swept over Funi Man and Koi Losa and carried with it a burning smell.

"What is that smell?" Koi Losa asked.

"Cedar," said Funi Man. "My house smelled like cedar in my dream. It burned to the ground—nothing left but cedar smoke."

"The witch knows we are here."

"Yes, Koi Losa. I think he knew as soon as we left Choctaw town. He is stronger than I thought."

"Do you still want to fight him?" Koi Losa asked.

"More than ever. Lil Mo cannot live long unless the owl dies."

"Hoke," Koi Losa said. "I understand."

"For now, we should not talk, not unless we have to," said Funi Man. He unrolled his blanket on the ground and turned to his saddlebag. When he finished unpacking, he motioned to Koi Losa and said quietly, "Help me make a fire circle."

Half an hour later, Koi Losa sat on a pine log by the fire. A small pot of water hissed and steamed and came to a boil. Koi Losa watched everything Funi Man did, looking for any secret signs or signals. He knew they were being watched.

Funi Man crouched by the fire with his head down. He dropped bits of bark into the water and spoke. "When the owl comes, he will come for me first. When you see him, do exactly the opposite of what you want to do. This is very important. The owl has already guessed what you will do. He knows you. He will be ready. Do the opposite, and we may have a chance."

Koi Losa said nothing in reply. He felt confused. He liked to plan his next move, but he could not, not with the owl. He had to wait, his least favorite thing to do in the world. He had to react to whatever the witch owl did.

And do the opposite of what I want to do? he thought. *How can I do that?*

The night crept along slowly, and Koi Losa felt confused by everything around him. He sat ten feet from the edge of a cliff. In the sky above him, owls flew from one tree to another, eyeing everything below.

Funi Man spent the evening by the fire, barely saying a word. Koi Losa gazed at the far wall of the canyon. Sharp rocks jutted out and thin trees twisted from among the boulders. Koi Losa winced at the thought of falling.

Just before nightfall he stepped to the edge of the cliff.

"Funi Man," he said, "I can see the bones of animals on the rocks below. It is a long fall."

"Let's try not to make it, hoke?" said Funi Man.

"I wonder what it was like for those animals, just before they hit the ground. It must be like flying."

"Koi Losa, be careful about your thinking. Keep your mind on what you have to do."

Koi Losa moved away from the cliff and sat by Funi Man. "You mean, remember to do the opposite?" he whispered.

"Yes. We have a chance to stay alive. I am depending on you to stay strong."

"Funi Man, I think I know what you mean. Finally I am understanding. About doing the opposite. It won't be easy, but I can do it."

"I am so proud of you," Funi Man said. "Whatever happens, always remember that."

"We are risking our lives, aren't we?" Koi Losa asked.

"Yes. We have a friend in danger, and we are helping him."

"We are going to be hoke, aren't we, Funi Man?" Koi Losa asked.

"Yes, Koi Losa. We might be changed, but we will be hoke. I should warn you, though. No one ever fights a witch and comes away unmarked."

Koi Losa nodded as they sipped their final cup of tea. Night sounds filled the canyon. They wrapped their blankets around themselves and lay back on leafy pillows.

Koi Losa tried every trick he knew to keep himself awake. He pinched himself in all the painful places. As his eyelids grew heavy, he rested on his elbows on the rocky ground. *That really hurts*, he thought.

When he did fall asleep, he felt something crawling

across his belly. He jerked awake and shook his head. Lifting his shirt, he slapped at a giant cockroach. He flung the cockroach into the air and heard the crackly fluttering of its wings.

Funi Man lay quiet as death, unmoving. He listened closely to every sound, every creak and flutter, every whistle and slither. Sleep was the smallest of his worries. He heard Koi Losa 's breathing, his restless tossing.

They both were wide awake when the owl man came for them.

CHAPTER 40

Owl at the Cliff

Funi Man had expected him to come from the dark swamp, or from the trees overhead. Instead, the owl man called from the opposite cliff.

"Hoooo! Hooo!" loud and floating through the foggy clouds, the witch owl called. "Squirrel Man and Panther Boy! How is your little slave friend, Lil Mo? He is already dead, you know. Burned up and black as ashes!"

Koi Losa jumped to his feet. "No!" He rolled his fists into tight balls of anger. "I will kill you! You're a mean and ugly witch!"

As he stepped to the edge of the cliff, his feet stumbled on the loose stones. Funi Man grabbed him by the shoulders, and they watched the stones fall to the boulders far below.

"Koi Losa, he had you," Funi Man said in a quiet and

soothing voice. "This is the witch's way. He is lying. You are stronger than this. I need you, and Lil Mo needs you."

"I am sorry," Koi Losa said. "You warned me, didn't you?"

"Yes, but we are still alive. All is hoke."

As they spoke, the witch man stood on the far cliff, stepping from one foot to the other. He hunched his shoulders and stomped his right foot, then turned in slow circles, chanting his song.

"Funi Man?"

"Yes?"

"Ilvppa ittibai foyuka."

"Yes, son. We are all in this together."

The witch spun faster, stirring dust at his feet. Feathers sprouted from his long sleeves and the base of his neck. He stopped with a suddenness that made Koi Losa gasp.

"Careful, Koi Losa," warned Funi Man.

The witch man's head, now the head of an owl, circled slowly on his shoulders. He raised an arm and pointed to the sky. Overhead, a bank of dark clouds appeared. They moved faster than any Koi Losa had ever seen. Low to the ground, they dipped into the canyon, splattering rain against the walls.

Everything disappeared from sight in the pounding rain.

"He is coming now," Funi Man shouted. "Koi Losa,

he is coming for us!" Koi Losa dashed for his blow-dart gun, and Funi Man picked up his shotgun. The rain was blinding. Funi Man waved his hand in front of his face and blinked.

"Hoooo!" came the cry, louder and closer.

When the witch finishes with Funi Man, he will come for me, Koi Losa thought. He jumped behind a tree, then peered slowly around the trunk. If he held his palm over his eyes, he could at least see shapes.

He watched as the witch owl took flight, spreading wings seven feet in length. His claws stretched out before him, larger than a man's hand. He lifted and lowered his wings and floated across the canyon.

The rain now fell in sheets. Water gushed from the boulders and down the cliff, washing like waterfalls down both sides of the canyon. But the witch owl's wings were dry. He flew through the rain, and not a drop of rainwater touched his feathers. With his claws thrust forward, he swooped from the sky.

He landed in the middle of the fire circle, and his wings were coated with a thin layer of ash. White and gray, he lifted his wings and hovered over the wet, dead embers of the fire. His yellow eyes shifted from one side to the other. His head turned.

"Hooo, hooo!" The sound was deep and surrounded Koi Losa, as if it came from the ground, the fog, the stones, the very air between the cliff top and the boulders below.

Where is Funi Man? thought Koi Losa. He dove into a clump of bushes and crawled across the ground.

"Where is the brave little Choctaw boy?" the witch asked. "Crawling on the ground? Yes, he is strong, that one!"

Koi Losa rolled to his knees. His clothes were caked in mud. With one hand he shielded his face against the rain, and with the other he moved the branches aside, looking through the tangled leaves and vines. He found Funi Man, leaning back against a thick tree stump. Funi Man held his shotgun pressed tight to his chest. He placed a finger to his lips, but Koi Losa knew to be quiet.

The witch owl lifted a clawed foot and pointed it at the stump. Funi Man stood and slowly walked to the witch. With every slow step he lifted the shotgun higher, till it rested easily on his shoulder, ready to fire. He paused and clicked the firing iron into place.

"Hoooo!" the owl called. "You think a shotgun can hurt me? Not before, not now!"

He arched his wings and swooped on Funi Man, his claws outstretched. Funi Man ducked and brushed aside a claw. His shirtsleeve ripped open, and a trail of blood flew from his wrist. The owl landed on the low branch of a pine tree and held his bloody claw high for Funi Man to see.

Funi Man backed away from the fire circle, and Koi Losa saw him nearing the edge of the cliff.

"Funi Man!" he yelled. "The cliff!"

The owl turned his head and looked at Koi Losa, but only briefly. He turned to Funi Man, who lifted the shotgun once more and fired, hitting the tree branch and causing the owl to stagger. In an explosion of bark and pine needles, the owl hurtled to the ground.

He landed in the ashes, and a gray cloud rose around him.

Koi Losa would never forget what happened next. He knew the owl was stunned. He knew the owl would ignore him and attack Funi Man with his dagger-sharp claws. Koi Losa also knew he could fire a blow dart at the head of the witch owl and hit him in the neck. The poison would kill him. He lifted the gun to his mouth and took a deep breath.

"You must do exactly the opposite of what you want to do," he told himself, repeating the words of Funi Man. "'Do the opposite, and we may have a chance.'"

"Help!" Koi Losa called out. Clutching his blow-dart gun, he dashed from his hiding place and ran to the woods.

"Hoooo!" screeched the witch. "Your brave helper is gone!"

Koi Losa took a quick glance over his shoulder and froze in his tracks. The witch owl stood in the fire circle with the legs of a man. His body and wings were those of the owl. He turned his owl head back and forth as he lifted his wings. Angered now, he ran quickly across the ground, waving his wings as he moved.

Funi Man backed up till his foot slipped on the cliff. He staggered, waving his arms for balance. His shotgun fell to the ground. The owl man spread his wings and lifted one leg. He aimed it at Funi Man's chest, to push him to the rocks below.

CHAPTER 41

Falling Body

Funi Man dropped to his knees and bowed his head. Unseen by the witch, he gripped the shotgun by the barrel.

"Hooo!" the owl screamed, already seeing the body of his Choctaw rival twisting and falling.

Funi Man did not fall. He grabbed the leg of the witch with one hand and jumped to his feet. Standing on one leg himself, Funi Man kicked the owl's wing upward with his other leg as he brought the shotgun down hard on the same wing.

Crack! A tuft of white feathers burst from the broken wing. Like a broken arm, the wing dangled and flopped. Funi Man swung again, knocking the witch owl to the ground. He struck the owl once more with the wooden stock of the shotgun and kicked him over the edge.

Koi Losa dashed from the woods and stood beside Funi Man. The owl screeched and screamed as he fell. His body became that of a man.

"You will die a broken man!" the witch shouted, just before he hit the rocks.

His neck snapped, and he hung backward over a block of limestone. His arms and legs twitched, but only for a moment. Owls flew from the treetops and rose to the top of the canyon. With a screech so loud that Funi Man and Koi Losa covered their eardrums, the owls flew off in all directions, and the witch lay still.

Koi Losa's chest pounded. He sat down hard as Funi Man looked to the sky.

"Yakoke, Holitopama," Funi Man whispered. He made his way to the fire circle, dragging his feet. With a thin pine branch he stirred the embers to life. Yellow flames flickered beneath the ashes, a trail of smoke rose, and the fire burst to life.

"Come here," said Funi Man, waving a tired hand at Koi Losa. "We're not finished. We can't leave his body here."

"What do you mean?" Koi Losa asked. "Animals will finish him off. Look!" Koi Losa pointed to the sky, where seven buzzards circled.

"We have to hurry!" Funi Man said. "The buzzards won't eat his bones, and somewhere among those bones is a lock of hair. Lil Mo's hair, remember. We will never know who finds it unless we bring it home with us."

"Oh, no," said Koi Losa. "We have to get it, don't we?"

"Yes, and we have to bring his body back with us. Shonti will know what to do, how to make it safe again for Lil Mo. And there is something else you should know, Koi Losa."

"What?"

"After what we have done, we are no longer safe, not yet. We must be very careful, son." Funi Man moved with urgency.

"Cover the fire with dirt," he said. "No need to try to hide the circle. Anyone can smell the fire and know someone was here. Let's just make sure the fire is out."

While Koi Losa loaded the saddlebag with cooking items, Funi Man wrapped his blanket in a tight bundle. "Follow me," he said. Taking his pony by the reins, he moved to a thick cluster of cedar trees a short distance from the fire, with Koi Losa close behind. They tied the ponies to a stout tree trunk.

"Easy, boy," Funi Man said in a soft and soothing voice. "We'll be back soon." Turning to Koi Losa, he added, "We need at least a hundred feet of strong vines."

"I know where to find them," Koi Losa said, pulling his hunting knife from its leather pouch. "I will meet you at the circle."

An hour later Funi Man and Koi Losa stood over the body of the witch. The vines dangled above them, weaving among the jutting rocks and boulders on the cliffside.

The old man was pale. His skin had claimed the whiteness of the owl. Feathers sprouted from his shirt collar, dotted with blood. Tufts of tiny white feathers emerged from his ears and nose. His eyes were the most hideous sight of all. They bulged from their sockets—black and yellow and bloodshot with thin red veins.

Funi Man reached for Koi Losa and wrapped his arms around him. As the two stared at the sight, Koi Losa's skin crept with a strange chill. The eyes of the owl protruded from the face of the witch.

"Death is hard to look at," Funi Man said, "and the death of a witch is the worst of all to see."

"Yakoke," Koi Losa said. "Yakoke for being here with me. I am afraid, but not like I would be if I were by myself."

"Ilvppa ittibai foyuka," said Funi Man. "Now, we have work to do." He unrolled his blanket and placed it on the ground beside the body. Lifting the witch's shoulder, he rolled him over and onto the blanket. Koi Losa stood back and watched.

"Help me with the legs," Funi Man said. "Careful where you touch."

Koi Losa took a deep breath and picked up one of the

witch's legs. It was thin and lightweight; he moved them both without struggling. Brown owl feathers poked from the bottom of the pants. One fell to the ground, and Funi Man stuffed it in the old man's boot.

"We don't want to leave anything behind," he said. "No telling who might pick it up, what they might do with it."

"If Lil Mo and I found an owl feather, we'd know to leave it alone," Koi Losa said. "Only one thing would make me more afraid."

"What would that be?"

"Paper money," Koi Losa replied. "I think it is maybe worse than owl feathers."

"Remember that when you grow up," said Funi Man, laughing as much as he dared.

CHAPTER 42

Blue Shawl Woman

Once the body was on the blanket, Funi Man tied both ends with a rope. He wrapped the loose end of a dangling vine around the witch's waist and pulled it tight.

"Think it's strong enough to lift him to the top?" he asked.

"I think so," said Koi Losa. "If we lift slow."

"Now," said Funi Man, "let's find another way to the top." He and Koi Losa walked along the creek bed for half a mile before the cliff dropped and became a steep, grass-covered hill. They glanced overhead and saw nothing unusual, no gathering of owls or flock of hungry buzzards.

"Looks like a good place to climb," said Funi Man. Soon, they stood overlooking the cliff. The witch still hung from the vine a hundred feet below. "I'll pull, and you watch out for any sharp rocks. We don't want to cut the vine and lose him."

He picked up the vine, wrapped one end around his wrist, and leaned backward, pulling on the vine.

"Looks good," said Koi Losa, as the body rose from the creek bed. He knelt and leaned over the cliff to get a better view. "No rocks in the way. Chim achukma?"

"Ahm achukma hoke," said Funi Man. "For now. He is lighter than I thought."

With the body halfway up the cliff, Funi Man asked, "Still hoke? No jutting rocks in the way? I can't see, remember?"

"I am watching," said Koi Losa. "All looks good."

Ten minutes later, Funi Man took a deep breath and gave a final strong yank on the vine. The body of the witch rolled on the ground at their feet. Funi Man dropped the vine and gulped for air. His chest heaved, and he grabbed his knees with both hands.

"I am too old for this, Koi Losa," he said. "The next time we kill a witch, you get to drag the body up the cliff!"

"I'll do it," said Koi Losa. Neither laughed. Funi Man's humor, they knew, was lost in the dark bundle that lay at their feet. Now they must carry this bundle through swamps, woods, and nahullo country.

Both Koi Losa and Funi Man stared at the body and shared a thought, though neither spoke it.

The witch is dead, but did Lil Mo survive?

"Let's get started," said Funi Man. "For now, I will drag the body behind my horse. When we get close to a town, we can carry it behind our saddles. We'll attract less attention that way. And if we trade out, the horses will stay strong. I'd like to ride as long as we can each day. Are you with me?"

"Ilvppa ittibai foyuka,"said Koi Losa.

"Achukma," Funi Man said. "Let's get home." He tied the vine to the saddlehorn and climbed onto Hawkeye. With Koi Losa following, they turned south, leaving the cliff and the fire circle far behind.

Avoiding main roads and towns, both Choctaw and nahullo, they moved swiftly through the pine woods. Koi Losa knew, without it being said, that his job was to look out for any followers. While Funi Man kept his eyes to the path ahead and the body behind, Koi Losa searched the treetops for owls.

Funi Man knew the land from times past, and by late afternoon they were halfway home. As they approached a swift-flowing stream, he pulled his horse to a halt.

"Let's take a short break," Funi Man said. "We can make the change here. Are you hoke with carrying him for a short while?"

"Yes," said Koi Losa. "I want to do my share."

"Trust me, Koi Losa, you have done more than your share."

Koi Losa felt a glow of pride and kinship with his friend. They stepped from their ponies and led them by the reins to the water. The ponies drank eagerly. Funi Man untied the witch bundle and wrapped the vine tight around Koi Losa's saddlehorn.

"Now, get yourself a drink, and I'll get us something to eat," he said. While Koi Losa knelt to the water, Funi Man took dried meat from his saddlebag. Soon they sat on the bank, sharing their meal and watching the ponies. Koi Losa scanned the surrounding woods and sky.

"One thing worried me about the body," Funi Man said. "I have thought about it all day and it makes no sense."

"What?"

"The buzzards," Funi Man replied. "Remember how the buzzards circled the body after the witch fell?"

"Yes, they flew close to him while we were climbing down the cliff."

"That's right, Koi Losa," Funi Man said. "But by the time we reached him, the buzzards were gone. I thought we might have to throw stones and send the buzzards flying, but they left on their own."

Koi Losa did not reply for a long moment. He knew what Funi Man was thinking.

"What would make the buzzards leave a dead man alone?" he finally asked.

"That is what worries me. Why *would* buzzards leave a dead man?"

They both stared at the body. The blanket was worn from being dragged up the cliffside and through the woods. The body now seemed curled and shriveled.

"It is a good blanket," Koi Losa said.

"Yes. I was hoping it wouldn't tear. We don't have another one. So far, it looks good."

"Funi Man, something is worrying me, too," Koi Losa said.

"What is it?"

"Do you know why I ran? When you were fighting the witch?" His eyes pleaded with Funi Man.

"Koi Losa, I understand why you ran. You were doing what I asked. The opposite of what the witch expected. You took his attention just long enough for me to pick up the shotgun without him seeing me. Don't worry about that!"

"Yakoke," said Koi Losa. "I was so afraid you would think I was a coward, I almost didn't ask."

"Koi Losa, you are doing more than most grown men would do. I respect you more every day."

The moment was interrupted by what they feared the most. With a soft rustling of leaves, a female owl landed in a nearby cypress tree.

"Time to be on our way," Funi Man said. "You get it

started, and I'll make sure the vine will hold, hoke?"

Koi Losa dragged the body for a short distance, and Funi Man rode around him, saying, "Achukma. Stay close and let me look for owls. You keep an eye on the body and where you are going."

As they rode away from the stream, Funi Man lost sight of the owl. Soon she reappeared, in a treetop half a mile away.

For the next two hours, the owl played a game, flying so close that both Koi Losa and Funi Man clearly saw her. She landed on the limb of a low-lying cedar bush, then rose high and disappeared. Soon they spotted her on the ground, fifteen feet in front of them, scattering leaves and scratching the dirt with her claws. As they neared, she flew away.

The sun dipped below the cloud line, and Funi Man held up his hand. He stepped away from Hawkeye and motioned for Koi Losa to do the same.

"As good a place to spend the night as any," he said. He cleared a patch of ground with his boot while Koi Losa gathered stones for the fire.

While they sat sipping tea and eating dried pork, Koi Losa said, "I didn't think you would want to light a fire tonight."

"No need to try to hide," Funi Man said. "The owls know where we are. The ponies need rest, and I don't want to travel at night." They finished the meal in silence. The embers burned low, and Funi Man leaned against a tree trunk, pulling his hat brim over his eyes. Koi Losa sat against a nearby tree.

Koi Losa heard her first and jumped to his feet.

"I didn't mean to scare you," said a woman's voice. She stepped into the dim light. "I thought I saw a fire and came to see who was camping on my land."

The woman wore a blue shawl wrapped tight around her shoulders. She was an older woman. Dark skin hung from her cheekbones, and her eyes were black. Funi Man rose to greet her.

"Halito," he said. "Chim achukma!"

Koi Losa tilted his head with wonder. *Why is Funi Man being so friendly?* he thought. *He's acting like he knows this woman!*

"Ahm achukma hoke, now that you are here," the woman replied. "I was hoping for somebody friendly when I saw the fire. I live by myself and get so lonesome."

"You have a house nearby?" asked Funi Man.

Koi Losa felt a chill. *If Funi Man does not know her, she knows him,* he realized. *She knows who we are.* He watched the woman closely. She wrapped the shawl around her face and her eyes turned to the blanket.

"Yes, my house is just through the trees," she said, still staring at the dead witch owl. "Why don't you young men come spend the night? No need to sleep on the hard ground." As she spoke, the leaves rustled, and the wind picked up. Koi Losa looked to the sky and caught a last glimpse of the moon before it ducked behind heavy rain clouds.

"We don't want to trouble you," said Funi Man, still in his friendly voice. "I might snore and keep you awake!"

"You are a funny man!" the woman said. The wind grew stronger, whipping her shawl from her shoulders. Koi Losa chased it into a clump of bushes.

"Here you are," he said shyly, returning the shawl.

"Please," the woman insisted, "let me take care of you both. You would make an old woman very happy." Fat raindrops began to fall, splashing in quick puddles on the forest floor. The embers hissed and smoked, and the ponies snorted.

"Your horses are welcome, too," she said. "I have a covered porch where you can tie them."

"I don't see how we can pass this up," said Funi Man. "I am thinking you were sent from the heavens!"

The woman did not reply. Funi Man shot a look at Koi Losa. For the first time, the young Choctaw realized this woman was not who she appeared to be.

CHAPTER 43

House of the Dead

"Koi Losa," said Funi Man, as if he'd read his thoughts, "Let's move! Bring the ponies. I'll carry the bundle."

The woman stepped aside and let Koi Losa and the ponies pass. She pointed to a narrow path, saying, "That way, son. Not too far." She slowly approached Funi Man, staying in the shadows and keeping her shawl pulled over her eyes.

Funi Man took his time with the dead witch. He tightened the ropes on either end of the blanket. "I will be along soon," he said to the woman. "Go on with the boy. No need for you to stay out in the rain."

"I don't mind," she said, still standing in the dark and staring at the blanket. "Can I help you?"

She doesn't want to leave the body, thought Koi Losa. *I am not leaving Funi Man alone with this strange woman*. He reached for his blow-dart gun and eased a poison dart into the hollow cane. Leaving the horses, he crept closer to the smoldering fire. Funi Man wrestled with the bundle, and for a brief moment turned his back on the woman.

Koi Losa watched as the woman eased the shawl from her head. She lifted her arms, and Koi Losa froze in fear. The woman changed before his eyes. A large owl woman now raised her wings and swooped on Funi Man, her claws outstretched.

Funi Man moved quickly. He raised his hands to his face and flung his fists at the oncoming owl woman. She staggered and stumbled, and Funi Man grabbed her by the neck. The owl woman sank a claw deep into his shoulder and raked it across his chest, sending a thick stream of bright blood down the front of his shirt. He dug his fingers into her neck feathers, revealing the smallest patch of white skin.

Koi Losa took a short breath and blew hard into the cane. The dart twirled and danced through the air, and sank deep into the neck of the owl woman. Her body twitched once, then dropped to the ground.

Still bleeding from the claw wound, Funi Man stood over the fallen woman. Her skin was wrinkled, and her hair was white and stiff as straw. As they watched, her feathers vanished. Her head fell backward, and her arms and legs sank into the soft mud. Koi Losa dropped his cane gun and fell to his knees beside the woman.

"Do not touch her!" warned Funi Man. "Koi Losa, don't feel bad about what happened. You did not kill this woman."

"I did," said Koi Losa, shaking. "I shot her with my blow-dart gun. But she was trying to kill you, Funi Man."

"I know you shot her. I gave you a small target, and you hit it, Koi Losa! Yakoke! Yes, you saved my life, but you didn't kill her."

"What do you mean?"

"Koi Losa, she was already dead. Dead and unburied. We came across her death place. The path through the woods maybe led to her old house, where she used to live when she was alive."

"How do you know this?"

"Look at her." The woman continued to shrink. Her skin turned to leathery flakes, which fell from her bones. Only her rib cage and a hipbone remained, poking up from the wet black earth.

A bolt of lightning crackled overhead, and in the flash of light they saw an old log cabin, sagging and rotting away.

"Look!" said Koi Losa. "That must be her house."

"Yes," said Funi Man, returning his gaze to the woman. "She probably died somewhere in the woods. I guess she lived alone. No one will ever know what killed her."

The rain fell harder, and more mud washed away, revealing a white leg bone and a cracked skull, missing most of the teeth. Funi Man knelt down and picked up the skull, and as he held it high, the rain suddenly stopped.

"The owl used her," Funi Man said. "He brought her back to life to use her. I don't think she was evil." He took Koi Losa by the arm and led him away. "Our business here is not over, not yet," he said.

Funi Man found the ponies where Koi Losa had left them, exhausted and waiting in a grove of pines. He tied the bundle to his saddlehorn and patted Hawkeye.

"Good boy," he said, as Koi Losa rubbed his pony behind the ears.

"They are good ponies for staying close," said Koi Losa.

Funi Man nodded. "Now, Koi Losa, we have a job to do," he said. "This woman is unburied. It is up to us to give her a good resting place."

For a long hour, Funi Man and Koi Losa dug up what remained of the woman. They scrubbed her bones clean and rolled them into a bundle, tied together with vines. While Koi Losa gathered cedar bark, Funi Man built a small fire. He lit the cedar and waved the smoke over the woman's bone bundle.

"Did you find a good burial place?" Funi Man asked.

"There is a tiny mound in back of the house," Koi Losa said. "Maybe someone in her family is buried there."

"Achukma," said Funi Man. "You lead the way. Carry the bundle, and we'll bury her."

Near the mound, Funi Man dug a hole with a stout pine branch. Koi Losa watched as fat sweat beads rolled down his friend's cheeks. Several times Funi Man stood up, leaned backward, and rubbed his back muscles.

"Funi Man, let me dig," he said.

"Yakoke," said Funi Man. "I guess I'm getting old."

When he finished digging, Koi Losa knelt and carefully laid the woman's bone bundle in the soft earthen hole. The two men stood and sang a slow chant.

"Funi Man," Koi Losa said, "I think I know what the old woman was after."

"What?"

"Lil Mo's hair. The witch man still has the leather bag with Lil Mo's hair in it."

"Koi Losa," Funi Man said, "I am growing more proud of you every day."

"Yakoke," Koi Losa said, taking a deep breath. The fear of witch owls and death left him, if only for a moment.

"It's been a long day," Funi Man said. "Let's get some sleep and try to make it home tomorrow."

Funi Man and Koi Losa spent the night under the sagging roof of the old woman's house, with a family of raccoons and a nest of barn swallows. They rose long before dawn and by sunrise were miles south of the woman's fresh-buried bone bundle.

As the sun climbed overhead, Funi Man lifted his hand, and they came to a halt. "Let's walk for a while," he said. "The ponies are working hard dragging the bundle. They need some rest."

They walked in silence for most of the day, stopping only for a quick meal of dried pork. Koi Losa needed a rest, too, but he said nothing. As they neared Choctaw town, thoughts of Lil Mo flew through his mind.

"Maybe someday we can look back and laugh at the past few days," said Funi Man, but he knew better. No laughter ever came from death. And though the witch was now a bundle on the ground, the hunt for the witch owl would haunt his thoughts forever.

They climbed a small hill, and the fields and homes of Choctaw town spread out before them. Funi Man scanned the treetops and his eyes settled on his own plot of land. A thin curl of smoke snaked through the trees surrounding his house. Koi Losa saw the smoke, too.

As they came closer, the smoke rose in thick, billowing clouds. Funi Man dropped the reins of his pony and ran down the slope.

"No!" he shouted. "Lil Mo!"

Koi Losa left the ponies and the witch man's bundle and followed. He overtook Funi Man halfway down the hill and reached the burning house first. The walls were aflame on all four sides. The cedar shingles of the roof were popping and bursting with fire.

Unaware of Funi Man's dream, Koi Losa stood and stared at the burning structure. A rafter crashed to the ground and he jumped back, covering his face from the swarm of hot ashes.

Funi Man pushed him aside and ran through the door, under the burning roof. "Lil Mo!" he screamed, his voice cracking with fear.

Before Koi Losa could follow, the entire roof crashed inward. A shower of burning boards and shingles scattered in a wide circle around the house. Koi Losa dove under the fallen roof and entered the cloud of fire.

CHAPTER 44

Not Without Scars

Koi Losa found Funi Man near the door, his leg caught beneath a rafter. He dragged Funi Man free, and they stumbled from the smoldering house, leaning against each other for support. When they reached a grove of trees a safe distance from the house, Funi Man slumped to the ground, clutching his knee.

"You saved my life, Koi Losa," he said, biting his lip in pain. "But Lil Mo is still in the house!"

"Funi Man," said Koi Losa, "you can't do anything for him, not now. I'll go for him. Wait here."

He circled the burning house. Logs fell, and the flames grew higher, casting a searing heat. Funi Man struggled to stand, then staggered to the flickering remains of his home. The smoke was thick, and he waved both hands in front of his face, coughing and lurching forward.

An explosion rocked the valley as the walls collapsed. Burning embers covered the sky and rained down on them. A thick log, red hot and smoking, rolled to Funi Man's feet and knocked him to the ground. Koi Losa grabbed Funi Man by the collar and pulled him away.

"Funi Man, if he is in the fire, Lil Mo is gone. We can't help him."

"No! I will not let him die! Shonti is with him!" The flames rose higher than the house ever stood. Funi Man looked to the sky, expecting to see owls settling in the nearby trees, witnesses to the final deed of the owl man on earth, the death by fire of Lil Mo and Shonti. He saw none.

"Do you hear him?" Funi Man asked, cocking his head and squinting.

"No, I can't hear him. He is gone, Funi Man."

"I hear his shilombish, Koi Losa. I hear his spirit. He is calling our names, Koi Losa. Lil Mo is calling our names. Not from the fire, but in the air. He is all around us, Koi Losa. Lil Mo is still with us. Listen!" he whispered.

Koi Losa listened and heard the voice, too.

The voice of Lil Mo floated closer and closer, till his whisperings were as clear as the fire before them. "I did this to you. I am sorry, Funi Man. Will you still be my Choctaw uncle?"

"Funi Man?" said Koi Losa.

"Yes?"

"Look behind you."

Funi Man turned to see Shonti and Lil Mo. Lil Mo was crying, and Shonti leaned over him, her arms wrapped around his chest.

"We left the house after midnight last night," said Shonti. "I had a terrible dream and knew we were not safe."

"I had the dream the day we left," said Funi Man. "I thought you were dead, both of you."

"The owl is gone," said Lil Mo. "I am Lil Mo again."

"Yes, the owl is gone," said Funi Man, pulling Lil Mo to his chest. "His body is rolled in a blanket." He pointed up the hillside to Hawkeye and the bundle behind him. "Shonti, we brought him to you."

"I know what to do," Shonti said. "And I have a corner of my house where you can sleep, Funi Man."

Before they spoke another word, they were surrounded by dozens of Choctaw men and women, drawn by the smoke and flames. Two men walked over the burning embers, kicking boards aside and looking at the charred remains.

"We should make sure the fire doesn't spread," said an elder woman. "One good wind and Choctaw town could burn. Bring water from the river!" she shouted.

Women clapped their hands, and children scampered. They returned carrying river-cane baskets filled with water. In less than an hour, every foot of ground surrounding Funi Man's home was dripping wet and under no threat to burn.

Friends of Funi Man lingered, sitting on logs alongside their saddened companion, and Lil Mo's family soon joined them. Mothers sent their children with bowls of pudding, and the older men visited while the fire burned low. The evening brought a soft breeze, and ashes rose from the smoky remains of Funi Man's house. Smoke curled from every corner.

"I guess I better be going to Shonti's," said Funi Man. Lil Mo and Koi Losa moved to his side. They had waited all afternoon, watching their elder friend prepare for a new life, a life away from home.

Funi Man stood up and moved in a halting, clumsy step, forgetting for a moment that he was injured. His young friends grabbed his elbows.

"You going to help your old friend?" Funi Man asked.

"You might be old, but you are still a funny man," said Lil Mo.

"Yakoke, Lil Mo," he said. "I wonder if I will ever be the same again."

Lil Mo and Koi Losa looked at each other without replying, but Funi Man already knew the answer. He remembered his words to Koi Losa as they began their journey.

No one ever fights a witch and comes away unmarked.

Koi Losa remembered as well. In the shadows of a cypress tree, he turned over his right wrist. For the first time, he looked at the blackened, bubbling skin of his forearm.

As he dragged Funi Man from the burning house, the rafter had flipped over and landed on his wrist. He fought to ignore the pain. The scar, two inches wide and almost a foot long, was his for life, and he knew it.

"No one ever fights a witch and comes away unmarked," he whispered to himself. An owl settled on a limb overhead, and the faint rustling of leaves disturbed his thinking.

"Koi Losa, I need you," Shonti called out. "Bring Hawkeye and follow me. Bring the bundle, too."

She means the witch owl, thought Koi Losa.

Shonti hurried away, and Koi Losa followed, leading Hawkeye by the reins. Trailing behind the pony, the owl man's blanket bundle bumped and tossed over logs and fallen leaves. When they reached Shonti's house, she pointed to a clearing among the pines.

"Untie the vine and leave the blanket there," she said. "You better get back to Funi Man."

Koi Losa left the body lying near a circle of stones. *She has her work to do,* he thought. *I wonder what will happen to Lil Mo's hair?*

Shonti entered her house and emerged with a red cloth bundle tied together with a small strip of yellow cloth. She unrolled the bundle, and several strips of cedar bark fell on the ground. Shonti lit a fire in the circle and held a long piece of cedar over the bright red flames.

When the cedar bark caught fire, she closed her eyes and moved it back and forth in front of her face. With her free hand, she waved the smoke to her nose. She closed her mouth, flared her nostrils, and breathed in the sweet cedar smells.

Shonti felt dizzy. She set the smoking cedar by the fire, and when she opened her eyes, the Choctaw everyday world was gone. Shonti now moved in the spirit world.

She was surrounded by people of every age—men and women, boys and girls. Some sat, some stood, some gathered in groups, but they all smiled at her.

"We are here because you called us," they said, though no words came from their lips. The words floated from the air, the trees, the earth itself. "We are here because you need us."

As quickly as they appeared, the spirit people vanished, but Shonti knew they never went away. They were always there, working for the good, helping those who remembered and walked in the light.

"Yakoke," she whispered.

Shonti felt a hand on her waist. She looked down to

see the eldest of her Bohpoli friends, four in all.

"Halito," she said, and the Bohpoli nodded.

Shonti knelt on the ground. She untied the vine rope and slowly unwrapped the witch man's bundle. Even before she saw the body, she was struck by the smell. The green-and-purple stench of death rose from the blanket. Shonti turned away and held her hands in front of her.

"Here, take this," said the Bohpoli, handing her the burning cedar bark. Shonti waved the smoking cedar over the bundle. Carefully, she pulled the blanket from the body, and what remained of the witch tumbled to the earth.

The owl man had shriveled during the two-day journey. His clothes were baggy and worn. His boots had fallen off during the trip, showing the callused soles of his feet. He lay chest up, but his head hung twisted backward, hanging by the frail bone of his broken neck.

Skinny hands poked through two torn and frayed sleeves. The fingers of one hand lay open, while the other hand was balled up in a tight fist.

"Lil Mo's hair," said Shonti, looking at the fist. She stood up and lifted her head to the sky. In a quiet voice she began singing. A soft whirring filled the air as six rattlesnakes slid from their lair. They surrounded Shonti, curling into a striking pose, and the Bohpoli disappeared.

Shonti clapped her hands and sang louder. The snakes

waved their heads back and forth to the rhythm of the chant.

The largest of the snakes uncurled and slithered onto the blanket. He crawled up the pants leg of the dead witch owl and wrapped himself around the skinny body. Thus protected, Shonti knelt once more and reached for the owl man's fist. Very slowly she unfurled the fist, one finger at a time. A small deerskin bag fell out.

She reached for the bag and felt a sharp claw dig into her palm. One finger of the witch man's hand ended in an owl claw. The pain was strong, but Shonti knew better than to flinch. She carefully pulled the claw from her palm and clutched the bag. She threw it into the fire and watched it burst into flames.

"That will be your last evil act on this earth," she said. With a stout cedar cane, she rolled the body into a nearby hole, six feet deep and already dug and waiting. The rattlesnake climbed from the hole as Shonti tossed burning logs over the body of the witch. Flames leapt ten feet high, lapping the low-hanging tree limbs.

Shonti backed away. She knew her rattlesnakes would guard the hole till every bone and patch of skin turned to ashes. The flames lit up the night, red hot and yellow.

Dark shadows flew over the hole as owls dipped back and forth through the flames. Though the trees hung heavy with the weight of owls, Shonti knew they had no power over her, not with the witch man gone.

"Spend the night if you like," she said aloud, "then be on your way. Your work here is finished."

With no more worry than a woman stirring a pot of pashofa, Shonti entered her house and went about the task of cleaning her wound. But she was not alone. Her Bohpoli friends boiled water and filled the bubbling brew with herbs. Shonti lay back, exhausted, as they performed their good, sweet medicine.

Outside, the flames flickered into harmless popping embers. Soon the once-powerful witch owl was nothing more than a pile of gray ashes at the bottom of a hole. The few remaining owls flew off into the night, and the moon shone bright as the sun.

With the witch owl gone from Choctaw town, Shonti enjoyed a restful sleep. She dreamed of Lil Mo and Martha Tom.

CHAPTER 45

Koi Losa and the Yannash

A week later

Koi Losa sprawled on the grass by the stickball field with his best friends and teammates. After a two-hour game, they were dripping with sweat and exhausted. Koi Losa told of his adventures chasing the witch owl.

"Start at the beginning," they urged him.

"The first day in nahullo town was the strangest day," Koi Losa said. "We traded six fox skins for iskuli."

"Iskuli?" asked Jonah, Martha Tom's cousin.

"Money, in nahullo talk," said Koi Losa. "Funi Man said we needed some, and he made the trade. Six fox skins for paper iskuli, paper money!"

At that moment Lil Mo walked up, and the group grew silent.

"Halito," he said.

"Halito," the boys said. They looked at one another and smiled. Since his return from the dark world of the witch owl, Lil Mo no longer spent all day with Koi Losa. More and more he was seen walking with Martha Tom.

"Where is she?" asked Jonah.

"Where is who?" said Lil Mo, pretending not to understand.

"Your puppy dog, Ofijo!" said Jonah, and they all laughed.

"Ofijo is a boy dog, and he is with Angel," said Lil Mo. "Why?"

"My friends were just wondering where you have been all day," said Koi Losa.

"No," said Jonah. "I was wondering where you have been all week."

Lil Mo shuffled his feet. "I've been helping Funi Man with his new house."

"That's funny," Jonah said. "He was here a minute ago, looking for you. We told him you were maybe with Ofijo. Or maybe Martha Tom."

"I was with Martha Tom, but she's mad at me now," said Lil Mo.

"That's too bad. Why is she mad?"

"I don't know. She gets that way sometimes. I always say the wrong thing."

"I can help you with her," Jonah said.

Lil Mo leaned against a tree trunk and tried to act uninterested.

"Well?" asked Jonah.

"Well, what?" asked Lil Mo.

"Do you want my advice?" Jonah asked, trying to hide his smile. The other boys, Koi Losa included, turned their heads and laughed quietly. "I'm her cousin. I know her better than anybody."

"I am tired of her," said Lil Mo. "I don't need help."

"Maybe you just need a place to hide!" another boy said.

"But if you do need help," said Jonah, "I know what will make her happy."

"What?" asked Lil Mo.

"Koi Losa was telling us about a sweet little bird he saw on his trip. It is called a yannash."

"A yannash?" Lil Mo repeated.

"Yes, that's good, Lil Mo," said Jonah. "Yannash. Say it again. Make sure you say it right. Yan-nash."

"Yan-nash," repeated Lil Mo.

Koi Losa didn't warn Lil Mo. He watched his friend fall into the trap, and even smiled a secret smile. *He has to learn somehow*, he thought.

"Just tell her she makes you think of a yannash," Jonah continued.

"Yes," said the second boy. "Tell her she looks like a yannash!"

"Even better," said Jonah, "tell her she *smells* like a yannash. They smell like wild roses. Martha Tom loves the smell."

"Will this make her happy?" asked Lil Mo.

All the boys nodded, all except Koi Losa, who rolled his eyes and looked away.

"What do you think, Koi Losa?" asked Lil Mo.

Koi Losa shrugged. "Jonah knows Martha Tom better than anybody," he said. *At least I am not lying*, he thought.

"Well, we should stop talking," said Jonah. "We're scaring all the fish away."

"Are you going fishing?' asked Lil Mo. "Where are your fishing poles?"

"We were thinking about fishing," said Jonah. "You want to go fishing with us?"

"Not right now," said Lil Mo. "I better go find Funi Man."

As soon as he was out of sight, the boys laughed long and hard.

"I better go find Funi Man," said Jonah in a singsong, mocking voice. "Did you see how his eyes lit up when I told him how to make Martha Tom happy?"

"He's got it bad," said Koi Losa.

"That was great!"

"Do you think he'll really tell her that?"

"Of course he will!"

"Can you see Martha Tom when he tells her she smells like a buffalo?" said Jonah. "I want to be there!"

"You could be a sweet little yannash and hide in the tree limbs!"

Lil Mo heard the laughter from a distance. "Hoke," he said to himself. "Let them laugh. I still don't want her to be mad at me."

He found Martha Tom husking corn on her back porch.

"Did you come to help?" she asked, without looking at Lil Mo.

"Uh, yes. Hoke. Let me help."

"You didn't come to help, so don't worry. You don't have to," she said, brushing dry husks from her hands and smoothing her dress.

"I just came to talk for a minute," said Lil Mo.

"Well, things don't always turn out so well when you just show up," said Martha Tom. "Remember when I cooked our first meal together and the real trouble started?"

"The meal was good," said Lil Mo. "Besides, it wasn't your fault about the witch man."

"I was scared for you. Do you know that, Lil Mo?"

asked Martha Tom. "Do you know how afraid I was that something would happen to you?"

"Funi Man and Koi Losa would not let anything happen to me."

"Every Choctaw in town likes your family," said Martha Tom.

"You, too?" said Lil Mo, looking to the ground and wishing he hadn't asked.

"Yes," Martha Tom said. "I like your family very much. Your mother and your father and your sisters, they are all very nice."

"Oh," said Lil Mo.

"What's wrong now?" asked Martha Tom.

"Nothing," said Lil Mo. "I was just hoping you liked all of us, because I want to tell you something."

"I should be getting back to work," said Martha Tom. "What is it you want to say?"

"You remind me of something," said Lil Mo, hoping he could remember how to say it. "Yan-nash, yan-nash," he repeated, whispering.

"What?" asked Martha Tom. "What do I remind you of?"

"You make me think of it, when I see you," he said. He looked over her shoulder, making sure her mother wouldn't hear him. "Martha Tom, you remind me of a yannash!"

"What?" she shrieked. She stood up and gave him a

threatening, one-eyed look. She put her hands on her hips. "I remind you of *what*?"

"A yannash," said Lil Mo. "And you have a sweet smell, just like a yannash."

"I smell like a yannash? Is that what you think?" she said, catching her breath in anger.

"Yes," said Lil Mo. "Don't be mad, not again, please. I am not joking. You smell like a yannash."

Martha Tom ran into her house. In a moment she reappeared with a bucket of dirty water. Lil Mo stood looking at her with his mouth open. Before Lil Mo could ask why, she dumped the dirty water on his head and dashed back inside, crying.

"What is wrong with you?" asked Ella, who was working in the kitchen. Martha Tom said nothing, and Ella stuck her head through the door.

"Lil Mo, what did you say to her?"

"I told her she smelled like a yannash, like a wild rose," said Lil Mo. "But I made her mad. I thought she liked roses."

"Lil Mo," Ella said, "a yannash does not smell like a rose. A yannash is a buffalo! You told Martha Tom she smelled like a buffalo?"

"Uh, no," stammered Lil Mo. "I mean, yes. I did. I thought it was a sweet little bird and smelled like a rose! She is really mad at me, isn't she?"

"Yes, Lil Mo, I think she is. Who told you about a yannash?"

"Jonah and his stickball friends," Lil Mo said. "Maybe they don't know, either."

"Lil Mo, Jonah knows what a yannash is," she said, laughing. "They had a good time with you!"

"I can't do anything right," said Lil Mo. "What can I do?"

"Lil Mo, you are dripping wet! Maybe you better just go home for now," she said. "Martha Tom will get over it. I will tell her you didn't know. Don't worry."

On his way home Lil Mo heard laughter coming from the bushes on either side of the path. "Who is it?" he asked.

"Wild roses," came the reply. Lil Mo didn't recognize the voices.

"Yes, Lil Mo. We are yannash. Don't we smell good?"

"Who are you and why are you making fun of me?" he asked. A bright green glow filtered through the leaves, and Lil Mo smiled for the first time all day.

"Where have you fellows been?" he asked. "I have missed you."

His Bohpoli friends stepped from the bushes and stood in the path before him.

"We have missed you, too, Lil Mo," said the elder. "We are glad to see you are safe and free of the witch man."

"Yakoke," said Lil Mo, "but I am in big trouble with Martha Tom."

"Can you blame her?" asked the smaller Bohpoli. "You told her she smelled like a buffalo!" The four Bohpoli laughed out loud, slapping their knees and gathering around Lil Mo.

"Lil Mo," said the elder, "anyone that can make a Bohpoli laugh is a good man. Maybe we can help you."

"How?"

"Well, your good friend Shonti makes the best love potion in all of Choctaw town. Just ask her. She can help you."

"Love potion?" asked Lil Mo. "What is that?"

"It is a drink, an herb brew, that will make Martha Tom like you, that's what it is!" the elder said.

"I could use something like that."

"Shonti is gathering herbs in the woods by Funi Man's old house. Just ask her. I'm sure she will help."

The green light dimmed, and soon Lil Mo was standing by the path alone. His friends were gone, but the laughter lingered, and from the bushes he heard, "Martha Tom smells like a yannash! That is the best love line I ever heard, Lil Mo. Good one, there!"

CHAPTER 46

Love Potions

Lil Mo made his way to what remained of Funi Man's house, where he found Shonti picking herbs in the nearby woods. The air smelled of burned and blackened wood, and gray ashes covered the leaves and plants.

"Where is Funi Man?" asked Lil Mo.

"I have given him a corner of my house to call his own," Shonti said, "at least until he decides what he wants to do."

"He must be sad about the fire," Lil Mo said. "Do you know what started it?"

"Not exactly, but I think the owl had something to do with it."

"How could he do that," Lil Mo asked, "when he was already dead?"

"Lil Mo, witches can do some things even I don't know about. I think this witch man was very powerful."

Lil Mo said nothing. He followed her from one plant to the next with his head hung low. Shonti soon realized he had a question he didn't know how to ask.

Probably not about witches and fires, she thought.

"Hoke, Lil Mo," Shonti said, "what kind of help do you need? You are in trouble with Martha Tom, am I right?"

"How did you know?" Lil Mo asked, jumping back in surprise. Shonti tilted her head to remind Lil Mo who he was talking to.

"Hoke. Yes," he said. "I told her she smelled like a yannash."

"You did what?" Shonti said. "Son, you do need help! What were you thinking?"

Lil Mo told Shonti how Jonah and his stickball friends had tricked him. When he finished, Shonti gave him a warm smile. She patted him lightly on the head and said, "Lil Mo, welcome to the Choctaw world. If your Choctaw friends didn't tease you, they would not be your real friends. They like you, Lil Mo. I know it doesn't feel like it now, but you and your family are very much loved in Choctaw town."

"Yakoke," Lil Mo said. "But Martha Tom doesn't like me. She's always mad about something I did."

"Far from it, Lil Mo. If she didn't like you, you could call her a buffalo or a smelly skunk and she would just laugh and walk away. She gets really mad at you because you matter to her."

"What can I do?"

"Lil Mo, I can make a brew that will make her see you like she has never seen you before. If she likes you now, she will adore you after she drinks the herbal brew."

"When could you have it ready?" said Lil Mo, trying to hide his excitement.

"Hold on a minute!" Shonti said. "I should talk to her mother first. I don't think they have chosen anyone for her to marry yet, but I want to make certain. I don't want anybody fighting over who gets married to whom!" Shonti smiled as she said it, trying her best to remember when someone she knew got married without a fight.

"Hoke," Lil Mo said. "Yakoke, Shonti. Maybe tonight, then?"

"Lil Mo!"

"Hoke, maybe in a few days?"

"I will let you know. In the meantime, why don't you spend your days with Koi Losa, like before?"

"What if Martha Tom forgets about me?"

"I don't think you have to worry about that," said Shonti, shaking her head. "You told her she smells like a buffalo and she dumped dirty water on your head. That's about as sure a sign of true love as I've ever heard!"

Lil Mo felt a nervous tremor run through him. He

wasn't so sure dirty water was a sign of love. *But after all, these Choctaws have some very funny ways!* he thought.

The next morning Koi Losa appeared while Lil Mo and his family ate breakfast on the porch. He waited in the tree shadows till Lil Mo spotted him. Lil Mo continued eating.

"Aren't you going to ask Koi Losa in?" Lavester asked.

"He probably already ate," said Lil Mo.

Lavester and Treda looked at each other without speaking. When Lil Mo finished eating, he walked outside. He waved at Koi Losa, and his hands began to move as he neared the tree where Koi Losa stood.

He pointed to himself. *I.*

He pointed to Koi Losa. *You.*

He tapped his chest with his fist. *Close friends.*

He drew a circle in the air. *Forever.*

He shrugged his shoulders and lifted his open palms. *Yes?*

You and I are close friends, forever. Yes?

Koi Losa walked slowly to Lil Mo and held out his hand. Lil Mo joined his friend in a strong and lengthy handshake with one hand, and a grip on the shoulder with the other.

"Ilvppa ittibai foyuka," Koi Losa said. "We are all in this together. Lil Mo, I'm not saying what I did was right."

"You tricked me, didn't you?" asked Lil Mo.

"Yes. It wasn't my idea, but I let it happen."

Lil Mo could have asked *"Why?"* He could have said, *"I thought you were my friend,"* or *"How can I ever trust you again?"* Instead, he waited for Koi Losa to explain himself.

"Every boy on our team gets tricked the same way, Lil Mo. I know nobody likes to be laughed at, but it's different with me and you and Jonah and our Choctaw friends. I think it is different for Choctaw grown-ups, too. We play jokes. We play them on everybody, even the councilmen and -women. It is part of the Choctaw way of living."

Lil Mo just looked at him, still waiting.

"Hoke," said Koi Losa, "who is your most respected friend, of all the Choctaws you know?"

"Funi Man," said Lil Mo, with no hesitation. "Everyone gets real quiet and listens when he talks."

"That's right," said Koi Losa. "And yet everybody laughs at him. Every day they laugh at him. He is Funi Man—Squirrel Man—but he is also a funny man. People respect him because he lets them laugh and joke about him."

"What does this have to do with me?" asked Lil Mo.

"Everything," said Koi Losa. "It is a test, Lil Mo. If you get mad and try to pick a fight or get back at the stickball team, then you are not a friend, not yet. You are not thinking like a Choctaw."

Lil Mo remembered jokes he and Joseph had played

on each other. "Hoke," he said, smiling.

"You have to admit," said Koi Losa, "it was a pretty good joke!"

"Uh-huh," said Lil Mo. "If it wasn't me, I'd be laughing. But will Martha Tom ever forgive me?"

"Lil Mo!" said Koi Losa. "You still don't understand! Martha Tom is crazy about you. You are all she talks about, don't you know that? That's why she is so mad!"

"But what if she thinks she smells like a buffalo?"

"Yeah," said Koi Losa, "and what if the first time you kiss her, she really does smell like one? What will you do then?"

"Hoke," said Lil Mo. "Let's just talk about something else." Without thinking, he wiped his mouth and spit on the ground. *What if she does?* he thought.

"Yuck! Buffalo breath smells bad!" Koi Losa said, throwing his arm around Lil Mo. "Let's go fishing!"

Lil Mo forgot to tell Koi Losa about Shonti's potion, and later that night he was glad he didn't. *This needs to be a big secret*, he thought. *No room for jokes, not with this.*

Martha Tom had one of the worst days of her life. She stomped when she walked. She stormed around the house, saying to herself, "I do not smell like a yannash!"

As she cleaned the corn, she flung cornhusks across the yard and against the wall of the house.

"What are you doing?" her mother asked.

"I'll pick them up later," she said. "I just need to throw something."

Years later she would refer to this as her Buffalo Day, while her mother called it Lil Mo's Dirty Water Day, but Martha Tom was too mad to laugh about it yet.

Funi Man came over for supper that night. Ella cooked grape dumplings, his favorite food. Funi Man had lived alone for all of his adult life, and now he had no home. After supper, the talk soon turned to Martha Tom's troubles with Lil Mo.

"Well, I guess I am not the only Choctaw with problems," Funi Man said.

Martha Tom folded her arms. She pouted and stomped on the floor. Everyone laughed. Even Martha Tom smiled for the first time that day.

"Hoke," she said. "Does Lil Mo even like me?"

"Of course he likes you," said Ella. "Shonti came by this afternoon asking if I had a husband in mind for you. I think she was asking for Lil Mo."

"What did you tell her? Mother, I am not ready for this!" Martha Tom said. She put her hands on top of her head and looked at the ceiling.

"Don't worry. I told her you were a little girl."

"Mother!"

"What did you want me to say?"

Martha Tom stomped her foot harder and stormed through the back door.

"Careful not to break a hoof!" yelled Funi Man.

Funi Man rose early the next morning and by sunrise was searching for herbs along the riverbank. Shonti already had her ingredients. With Funi Man gone, she began boiling water for Lil Mo's potion. By late morning, Funi Man returned to Shonti's house and smelled the steaming brew.

"What are you cooking?" he asked, hiding his basket of herbs under his bed.

"Nothing important. Just herbal tea in case anybody wants some," Shonti replied.

"I hate herbal tea!" said Funi Man.

"Good. Then I can have it all for myself," said Shonti. She soon lifted her boiling pot of tea from the fire and moved it to the windowsill to cool. "Behave yourself, Funi Man," she said. "I am going for a walk."

As soon as Shonti was gone, Funi Man placed his own herbal brew on the flames and waited for it to boil. The rising steam and sweet aroma from Shonti's brew caught his attention. "Ummmm, smells sweet," he said. "I might have a taste when it cools."

As the sun rose in the afternoon sky, Funi Man felt his

age. He had spent all morning bending over, kneeling and crawling through bushes and gathering herbs. His knee throbbed, and his back hurt.

"Time for an old man nap," he said. "Maybe Shonti's tea will help me sleep." He lifted the bowl from the window and carefully carried it to the base of an old oak tree nearby.

He leaned against the tree and stretched his legs, rubbing his throbbing knee. "Maybe it's cool enough. I'm sure Shonti won't mind."

He slowly lifted the bowl, blew across the sweet tea, and took his first sip. Setting the bowl to the ground, he closed his eyes and let his head fall to his chest—expecting an easy afternoon nap.

How wrong he was.

As the warm brew of Shonti's herbal tea flowed down his throat, Funi Man awakened. He felt the warmth flow from his chest to his fingertips. He took a deep breath and opened his eyes wide. The world was no longer hot and tiring. The sky was a beautiful blue, the trees waved with the rhythm of a song, and Funi Man felt twenty years younger.

He quickly picked up the bowl and gulped down the remaining tea. "Achukma! Good day today. Good life from this day forward."

He rose to his feet and gazed across the valley, across

the waters, looking for adventure. His wish was granted as he spotted Shonti stepping from the woods and heading home.

"How could I not have seen the beauty of this woman—Shonti? Sweet and tender and round as a rosebud."

An idea struck him, so strong he bounced against the tree trunk. "I know what I must do," he whispered. "Yes! And quickly!" He dashed to the house and poured his herbal tea in a cup of warm red clay.

"Shonti!" he shouted, as she neared the house. "I made a cup of tea for you. Please, will you be so sweet as to taste it? Let me know if you like it."

"Funi Man? Is this another crazy Funi Man joke? What's going on?"

"Just sip the tea, please. No joke. I promise."

Shonti shook her head in wonder. "Hoke," she said. "Give me the cup, but if this is a joke, I'll call my rattle-snakes. I'm warning you!"

Funi Man said nothing. His wide eyes stared at her, touching every inch of her soft skin. As she sipped the tea, Shonti spotted her empty bowl, lying by the tree trunk. *Funi Man drank the herbal tea! He is falling in love. With me!*

She swallowed every drop of tea, then dropped the cup.

CHAPTER 47

Wedding Plans

News of the impending wedding of Funi Man and Shonti soon had Choctaw town in the throes of laugher. In the days leading up to the wedding, people smiled more than ever. People woke up laughing for no reason, even serious-minded people.

"Why are you laughing?" wives asked their husbands, but no one ever answered that question, or if they did, no one heard them. They were too busy laughing. Every Choctaw felt like they now had permission to do the silliest, funniest things they could imagine. Just like Funi Man!

Children dug up worms from the riverbank and dangled them from their fingers, wondering where would be the funniest place to put them. Older brothers caught harmless snakes and wondered who needed them in their beds the most. Husbands scared their wives with handmade claws, and wives hid beetles in their husbands' britches.

Four days after Funi Man sipped Shonti's brew, the Choctaw council met in a special short session, called by Hattak Chula. Koi Losa and Lil Mo sat outside the council shelter, along with a hundred other Choctaws, and listened to the meeting called to discuss the wedding.

"Let us talk about this wedding," Hattak Chula said, opening the meeting.

"Which wedding?" asked Blue Doe, and everyone laughed.

"The traditional wedding might not work here," said Hattak Chula, ignoring both the question and the laughter. "The bride is always given a head start in her run to the wedding pole, as you know. If she reaches the pole before the groom catches her, the wedding is off."

After a long pause, Blue Doe asked, "What is the problem?"

"Funi Man is older than any groom I can ever remember," Hattak Chula said, "and I am an old man."

"Yes?" Blue Doe asked.

"Well, as an old man," Hattak Chula said, "I cannot see myself dashing across a field after a woman, racing her to a pole with everybody in town watching."

"So," asked Blue Doe with a smile, "if you had not met

your wife till you were an old man, you would not think she was worth running after?" Everyone in the council tried to hide their laughter, but only for a moment. When Hattak Chula stumbled trying to reply, they laughed along with everyone else.

"Of course I would run after her!" he declared.

"Well, you wouldn't catch me, not if we had to do it again!" said his wife, slipping through the crowd and entering the shelter.

"Where did you come from?" asked Hattak Chula.

"I followed you here," she replied. "Blue Doe told me I might want to be here."

"You tricked me!" said Hattak Chula, turning to Blue Doe.

"So," asked Blue Doe, "can an old man run or not?"

"Of course, if his love is true!" said Hattak Chula, having learned his lesson. "I would crawl on my knees to marry my lovely wife!"

His skinny bride of forty-seven years folded her arms and tightened her lips. "You'd better!" she said.

"Then we can have a traditional wedding, with no special favors for Funi Man?" Blue Doe asked.

"Funi Man with the limping leg?" asked Hattak Chula. "Yes, hoke, we will all gather to watch Funi Man try to catch Shonti." He frowned, knowing his friend Funi Man would be the joke of his own wedding day.

Then the frown left his face. He smiled and finally laughed out loud.

"You are right!" he declared. "Who deserves laughter on his wedding day more than our very own Funi Man!" The Choctaws cheered and laughed, and men lifted anyone light enough to throw. In a show of strength, several women even lifted their skinny-boned husbands!

"Should we warn Funi Man?" Koi Losa asked.

"What good would that do?" Lil Mo replied. "He is in love. I never had a chance to give the potion to Martha Tom, but Funi Man is getting married! How did this happen?"

Deep in the swamps, at the bottom of a warm hole, four Bohpoli enjoyed a warm stew for breakfast.

"What a time we've had!" said the eldest. "I haven't slept for a week!"

"None of us have," said another. "Between Funi Man and Shonti . . ."

" . . . and Lil Mo and Martha Tom . . ."

" . . . and Koi Losa and—"

"Wait! Koi Losa! We are forgetting about Koi Losa!"

"Yes," admitted the elder Bohpoli, "we are forgetting about Koi Losa, and we will continue to forget about Koi Losa. Let him have some peace. He can fall in love later."

"Besides," said another, "we need a little peace ourselves."

"Even Bohpolis need sleep!"

But sleep was not in the offing for the Bohpolis, for the wedding day was nearing.

———

As he did every Sunday, Joseph stood at the crossing place, hoping to see his friend. Weeks had passed with no Lil Mo. Joseph often wandered by the river before sunrise, when he would not be seen. Sometimes, as the sun fell behind the thick cedar groves on the Choctaw side, he stood and stared at the moon. When the full moon waned, he felt Lil Mo growing further and further away from him.

"Friends forever," he often recalled. "Lil Mo and Joseph, friends forever."

Without thinking or realizing what he was doing, Joseph sometimes threw a stone across the river to the shady shore where Lil Mo used to stand.

On the final Sunday before the wedding day he tossed a stone, and when he looked up, there stood Lil Mo! Within half an hour, Joseph pulled Lil Mo's boat ashore.

"I brought Ofijo," Lil Mo said. "So I probably better not stay long. I knew you'd want to see him."

"Thanks," said Joseph. He smiled so big Lil Mo laughed.

"You look like a happy possum," Lil Mo said. "Grinning and grinning!"

"I feel like a happy possum!" Joseph said, laughing. "It's good to see you!"

"Why don't you climb in my boat? Let's cross over. Shonti and Funi Man will want to see you!"

"Good idea!" Joseph said. "Where have you been? I've been worried."

"I've had a hard time. A witch owl came into town, and I was sick for a while."

"Sick?"

"Well, even worse than that," said Lil Mo. "Come aboard and I'll tell you about it, at least what I remember."

"You are talking in riddles," said Joseph, climbing into the boat. "What happened to you?"

"Funi Man can tell you better than I can," said Lil Mo, pushing the boat into the river. Ofijo barked and leapt into Joseph's lap.

"Good boy," Joseph said. "Good to see you. Did you miss me?"

Ofijo snapped a friendly bark and licked Joseph on the cheek.

"I think that means yes," said Lil Mo. When the boat landed, he jumped out and dragged the boat to a thick clump of bushes, covering it with pine boughs. "Now, let's find Funi Man," he said.

"So other than you and this witch owl, what's been going on in Choctaw town?" Joseph asked.

"Hoke, are you ready?" said Lil Mo. "Funi Man and Shonti are getting married!"

"I thought they were too old to get married," said Joseph.

"Love knows no age—at least that's what Funi Man tells me. I'll let him tell you himself. He's not the same old man he was before."

As they approached Shonti's house, Lil Mo lowered his voice before speaking. "Funi Man's house was burned to the ground," he said. "We think the witch had something to do with it."

Joseph stopped. "Lil Mo," he asked, "are you all right? What are you not telling me?"

"I am all right now," said Lil Mo. "But this witch was a man who changed into an owl. I know it sounds crazy. Joseph, I saw everything through the owl man's eyes. For several days I trusted no one. I am glad you didn't see me then."

"You know I would have done everything I could to help you," said Joseph. "Lil Mo and Joseph, friends forever. Remember?"

"Of course I remember," Lil Mo said, with a deep breath and a smile. "Still true. Lil Mo and Joseph, friends forever."

"Wait, Lil Mo," said Joseph. "Did I hear you say Funi Man was marrying Shonti? Rattlesnake woman Shonti?"

"Shhhh!" said Lil Mo. He looked over his shoulder and grabbed Joseph's arm. "We don't call her that, not on this side!" Lil Mo laughed out loud. "Joseph, things are different here, more different than I ever thought. We have a lot to talk about!"

As they entered Choctaw town, the sound of chanting filled the street.

> *Ya da hada yamma,*
> *Ya da hada yamma,*
> *Yada hada yamma,*
> *Yada ha ya ma!*

"The friendship chant," said Lil Mo. "They sing it all day long now. This is a happy time for Choctaws. Two of the elders are getting married."

"Lil Mo," said Joseph, with a shy tremble in his voice.

"What is it?"

"Can a nahullo come to the wedding? I want to be there!"

"Would you? Yes!" Lil Mo shouted. "Of course you can come! This is great news!"

"I have to ask first," said Joseph. "Would it be safe?"

"Yes," said Lil Mo. "No Bledsoe. No witch owl. You would be safe, I promise."

"And no rattlesnakes?"

"I can't promise that," said Lil Mo.

They soon approached Shonti's house, and Lil Mo stood outside the door. "Shonti, can we come in?" he asked. "It's me, Lil Mo, and I have my friend Joseph. Is it hoke to come inside?"

Shonti was gone, but Lil Mo pushed open the door and found Funi Man sleeping behind a curtain in his corner of the house. "Funi Man," he shouted, shaking him gently. "When did you put a curtain up?"

"Uh, halito, Lil Mo," said Funi Man, waking up and smacking his lips. "Shonti said I should not see my bride till after the wedding."

"You can't see her? How do you do that? You two live in the same house."

"Yes," said Funi Man. "It is not easy. I have to call out for Shonti to hide herself whenever I step out from my tiny little corner."

"Men sure do a lot for love," Lil Mo observed.

"More than you'll ever know," agreed Funi Man. "Well, maybe not more than *you* will ever know."

"Yes," said Lil Mo, "if I remember right, this whole wedding started off because of me and Martha Tom."

"That seems like a lifetime ago," Funi Man said.

"But look who came to visit!" Lil Mo shouted. "Joseph, come here!"

Joseph eagerly stepped around the curtain.

"Joseph!" Funi Man said. "Great to see you, son. Will you come to the wedding?"

"I hope so," Joseph said, smiling and shaking Funi Man's hand.

Funi Man's eyes still had a strong spark of life, but they now harbored something else as well—the pains of old age. His hair was grayer since chasing the witch owl, and his face held wrinkles that had only been tiny lines before the journey.

When Funi Man stood to greet Joseph, his hand went immediately to his right knee. He rubbed it with his thumb for a moment, saying, "I guess Lil Mo told you about the owl man?"

"Yes," said Joseph. "He told me everything he knew."

"Funi Man," Lil Mo asked, "can we go outside and talk? About everything that has happened?"

They sat beneath the wide spread of an old oak tree. Funi Man boiled water over a fire circle. He took dried leaves from a pouch and sprinkled them over the water. "Lil Mo, can you bring three cups from the house?"

At that moment, Koi Losa appeared in their midst, jumping down from a limb just over their heads.

"Better bring four," Funi Man said quietly. Nothing Koi Losa did surprised them anymore.

They waited without speaking. Funi Man poured the

tea. He closed his eyes and sang a low chant, a blessing for the teaching moment to come.

Funi Man looked at Lil Mo, Koi Losa, and Joseph. "You are waiting for a story," he said, "a teaching story from your old friend Funi Man."

They nodded and waited.

"I remember my grandfather, my Choctaw amafo. I remember as clearly as if it happened this morning, the morning when I came to visit him. After breakfast he patted me on the shoulder and led me outside to a circle of stones behind his house. Thick logs surrounded the stones, and we sat down close to each other.

"He said to me, 'You are waiting for a story, a teaching story from your Choctaw grandfather.' I nodded and waited. He said to me what I will now say to you.

"My days of teaching and telling stories are over. Your time has come. I am passing the stories to you, and you must carry them and pass them on."

The afternoon sun settled behind the pine trees, and long shadows stretched across the clearing. Lil Mo, Joseph, and Koi Losa sat without speaking for a long moment. Lil Mo and Koi Losa looked at each other. Their friend was growing older. Funi Man had shared a memory that few living Choctaws knew. For the first time, Koi Losa and Lil Mo realized that Funi Man needed them. He always seemed the strong one, the teacher.

"Can I tell you what you are thinking?" Funi Man asked.

"Hoke," said Koi Losa, and Lil Mo nodded. Neither laughed, as they would have a month ago.

"You are thinking something I have known for a long time. The day will come when I depend on you, both of you. Maybe you, too, Joseph. Maybe that day is already here."

Together, as if they spoke in the same voice, Koi Losa and Lil Mo repeated words they had learned from Funi Man, their teacher. He would remember this moment as one of the proudest of his life.

"Ilvppa ittibai foyuka," they said. "We are all in this together."

"Yes," said Funi Man. "Ilvppa ittibai foyuka."

"Funi Man," Lil Mo said quietly, "are you happy? Can you be happy again?"

Funi Man shook with soft laughter. "Yes, I am very happy, happy in a quieter way. I am happy seeing the dried leaves fall from this old red oak tree. I know they will wrinkle and crack and sink into the ground. Some new plant will take the leaves as food and grow strong. I don't have to do anything. That happens whether I am here or not."

"Turn your head and close your eyes, Funi Man!" Shonti called from the house. "Somebody has to cook around here, and I guess you men just want to talk. I am setting a pot of tobi walhali on the porch."

"Boiled beans!" Lil Mo said. "I am hungry!"

"I see you've not forgotten your English!" said Funi Man.

"Now that's funny," Lil Mo said, glad to be with his friend again. "Come on, Joseph!"

The boys helped Funi Man to the porch, where four bowls, four spoons, and a steaming pot of tobi walhali waited for them.

"Lil Mo," Shonti whispered to Lil Mo, "I made some banaha bread, too. I know Funi Man loves bread cooked in the corn shucks. Is he all right?"

"He is good, and he'll be better after the wedding."

"I think he misses seeing you," said Joseph.

"He will just have to wait," Shonti replied. From behind the door came the whirring sound of a rattlesnake. Joseph shivered and looked to Lil Mo for help.

"Hoke," said Lil Mo, "we understand!"

CHAPTER 48

Surprise for Lil Mo

On the wedding day of Shonti and Funi Man, every Choctaw with legs, and some without, circled the field and waited. Shonti and Funi Man had thousands of friends, and no one wanted to miss their wedding. Everyone knew this would be an unforgettable Choctaw day.

Bright colors gave a festive air to the gathering. Women wore their finest dresses; red and blue and green skirts swirled and swayed. Men wore brightly colored shirts, too, with diamond-back rattlesnake designs crawling down the sleeves.

"Am I seeing what I think I'm seeing?" Lil Mo asked, as he and Koi Losa and Joseph approached the gathering.

"What do you think you are seeing?" asked Koi Losa.

"I see snakes wrapped around women's dresses and men's shirts. Tell me I'm wrong. Please."

Koi Losa laughed loudly, saying, "Lil Mo, you have seen a wedding before, remember?"

"That seems like another life, before I became Choctaw," said Lil Mo.

"Choctaw women sew the rattlesnake diamonds on the nicest clothes," Koi Losa said. "Ask Funi Man why. He'll have a better answer than mine."

Joseph walked in silence, with his jaw dropped and his eyes wide, staring at everything. "This is the biggest holiday I've ever seen in my life," he finally said.

"We are glad you are here with us," Koi Losa said. As he walked between his two newest friends, Koi Losa smiled in thought. He looked to his left, at Joseph, the son of a slave guard. To his right walked Lil Mo, the son of slave parents.

And here I walk, he thought, *like never before. We walk together on this sacred day, so different by our skin, yet so alike in so many ways.*

Reverend Bob, the Choctaw preacher, neared the stickball pole, where the service was to take place. The crowd grew silent. A small hut of thick leaves and branches, built only yesterday, sat at the far end of the field. Shonti sat inside the hut, behind a leafy door and surrounded by women friends, as six rattlesnakes quietly nestled nearby.

Koi Losa led his friends behind the hut. They greeted Funi Man and sat beside him on a thick log.

"Did Lil Mo tell you about how the wedding goes?" asked Koi Losa.

"Yes," said Joseph. "Funi Man will catch Shonti before she reaches the stickball pole. Then the wedding happens."

"If she wins the race and touches the pole first, the wedding is off," said Funi Man.

"Not happening," said Koi Losa, smiling, "and you know it, Funi Man. A Choctaw wedding is mostly a funny game."

"Just right for a funny man!" said Lil Mo.

"And you think that's funny?" asked Funi Man.

Joseph was about to ask, *When does the race start?*, but the words never left his mouth. The leafy door at the front of the hut opened, and the crowd of Choctaws jumped up and down, shouting, "Shonti, balili!"

But Shonti did not exit the hut. To everyone's surprise, Martha Tom sprinted through the door. She wore a soft cotton dress with blue diamonds on the sleeves. Her hair flowed behind her as she ran, lean and quick, pumping her strong arms and splitting the wind.

"Martha Tom!" A cheer rang out across the grounds. "Balili, Martha Tom!"

"What?" Lil Mo asked. "Why are they cheering for Martha Tom?"

Koi Losa leapt from behind the hut and glanced ahead.

"Balili, Lil Mo! Balili!" he shouted, pointing to the front of the hut. "Martha Tom is fast. You better hurry!"

"What is happening?" Lil Mo shouted.

"Don't ask," said Koi Losa. "Just run! Balili!"

Lil Mo jumped to his feet and turned first one way, then the other. Everyone in the Choctaw crowd pointed to Martha Tom, laughing and yelling and slapping their cheeks in amazement.

"There! Hurry!" The shouts and calls were more than the morning could hold. Lil Mo ran to the front of the hut in time to see Martha Tom circle the pole and reach out her hand, but at the last moment she turned like a whirlwind and ran to the woods.

Lil Mo stood, unable to move.

"She is so beautiful," he said aloud. Everyone clapped and cheered at the sight of their very own Martha Tom, dashing in and out of the trees, to the pole again, circling the pole but never touching it.

But as Martha Tom ran with grace and beauty, Lil Mo had the speed to match her. Koi Losa slapped him on the shoulders, and he sprang to life. He gripped his fists and opened his palms back and forth as he ran. His legs churned beneath him, legs lean with muscle. He almost caught her as she made her second pass at the wedding pole.

When Lil Mo realized the dance was a game for all to see, he made every Choctaw proud that he was now among them. He dove for Martha Tom, his future bride. He dove for the hem of her dress.

Lil Mo flew through the air like a raven, a dark and kingly bird. Martha Tom froze to see the joy on his face. No one would ever know if Lil Mo missed catching her by his own design, or if she spun on her heels at the last moment, away from Lil Mo and into the woods.

With all eyes on the young runners, Shonti slipped quietly from the hut and walked toward the pole. She lifted her chin and moved in dignity. She was twenty feet from the pole when the men began to yell.

"Balili, Funi Man! Balili! Run!"

Funi Man was caught by surprise. He flung his arms at Koi Losa. "Help me," he shouted. "Help me get up!"

Koi Losa grabbed him by the wrists and hoisted him to his feet. Funi Man slapped his right knee awake and took a giant stride with his left leg. His right leg refused to follow.

Funi Man fell on his face. The women clapped and cheered. Shonti waved and tilted her head at her admirers, thinking they were cheering for her. When she saw everyone pointing at the old man she had grown to love, her hands flew to her face.

"Oh, Funi Man," she shouted. "Stay where you are. I am coming for you!"

"No!" the men shouted. "You can't do that! He must

catch you on his own, or the wedding is off."

Funi Man rolled to his feet and tried to stand. Koi Losa ran to his side and lifted him by the waist.

"Can you make it?" he asked.

"Of course," Funi Man said in a whisper, "but don't let Shonti know. She likes to take care of her old man, and this is her day, so let her do it."

"But she will touch the pole, and then you can't get married," Koi Losa replied.

"Son, you don't know her like I do. She is the sweetest, stubbornest woman in all of Choctaw country. She'll never touch the pole without me. A hundred rattlesnakes couldn't drag her to that pole!"

Funi Man was right. Shonti stopped ten feet from the pole. She slowly lowered herself to the ground, brushed the hair from her face, and began to pick tiny flowers from the grass at her feet.

The Choctaw crowd was a sky of dancing clouds in a spring windstorm. Some laughed so hard they cried. Others jumped up and down and fell on top of each other, grabbing neighbors and kinfolk and even total strangers. Some stepped back and shook their heads in wonder. Older men and women simply held one another at the beauty of the spectacle before them.

Funi Man limped and dragged his leg behind him, stumbling twice before he fell for the final time at

Shonti's feet. She leaned over and kissed him, and though everyone wanted to cheer, none did. They were too tired by this time.

"Shonti and Funi Man," they said in voices hoarse from the madness.

Lil Mo and Martha Tom stepped from the woods and joined their elders, making a circle of four around the wedding pole.

The women wedding dancers gathered slowly, rising like ducks from a glassy lake in the woods, a lake known only to Choctaws. The men moved like white-tailed bucks, some old, some young. Silence settled over the grounds. Four robins flew from a pair of pines growing close to the field, bright red-breasted robins, dipping low to bless the wedding.

The dancers joined hands, and the ceremony began. Chant sticks snapped out their wooden rhythm, and deep voices sang the Choctaw wedding chant.

When the chant was over, Hattak Chula stood and placed his hands on Lil Mo's shoulders. "Welcome to your new family," he said in a voice as deep as the spring.

He turned to face the crowd, closing in tight around the four.

"Martha Tom is promised to Lil Mo, and they will be wed at the Green Corn Ceremony when they're grown up," he declared. "Her mother has agreed. Lil Mo has shown his wish in many ways, and we will honor this marriage."

He then turned to Shonti and Funi Man.

"Join the Choctaw council and me on this most happy day for all Choctaws. Two of our elders are marrying here today."

Reverend Bob, the tribal pastor, lifted Shonti's hand and that of Funi Man. He closed his eyes, turned his face to the sky, and blessed the couple in a deep voice, loud enough for all to hear.

Following the ceremony, everyone turned to tables scattered among the surrounding trees. Choctaw women had cooked for days leading up to the wedding. Steaming soup, crispy chunks of meat, and sweet puddings covered the tables.

———

Unseen by the celebrating Choctaws, a small boat crossed the Bok Chitto River a mile north of town. "I have landed here before," said Harold, pulling the boat to the base of a giant cedar tree.

"You were right about everyone being at the wedding," Bledsoe replied. "No guards saw us cross the river."

"Can we bring our guns when we land?" Harold

asked. "And thank you, Mr. Bledsoe, for returning my shotgun."

"Let's leave our shotguns here," said Bledsoe. "We know where they are if we need them."

Harold turned away from Bledsoe and made an ugly face. He did not like leaving his gun behind.

"I will carry my pistol," Bledsoe said. "And my hunting knife and whip."

CHAPTER 49

Bledsoe in Choctaw Town

"How long do we have before the wedding is over?" Harold asked.

"The feast might last till morning," Bledsoe said, "but we should be gone in two hours. Now, let's get going."

When they reached the top of a small hill, Bledsoe pointed to a wide cornfield. "Look," he said. "This land is already cultivated—hundreds of acres of river bottom soil. Can you imagine what these fields will look like, white with cotton?"

"I'll love to see it," said Harold.

"You will," said Bledsoe. "You will."

They crossed the field of cornrows and climbed a hill to the west.

"Look," said Bledsoe, pointing to a lake, glowing

golden in the moonlight. "I've always known that Choctaws have the best land. Yes, we will have some fine cotton fields when we own it."

Shonti and Funi Man sat in a grove of red oak trees, surrounded by cheerful Choctaw friends. Shonti held a bowl of pudding. She was lifting the spoon to her mouth when she felt an itching. It started at her ribs and inched across her belly. She slapped herself and grimaced.

"What was that?" asked Funi Man.

"I don't know. Something stung me!"

The itching grew to a burning, as if a scorpion was sinking its stinger into her skin, taking tiny steps, and stinging her again and again.

"Funi Man," she said, "something is happening. Someone is crossing my land."

"Are you sure?" asked Funi Man. "Maybe it's the excitement of the day."

"No," she said, gripping his arm hard. "Funi Man, I am feeling dizzy."

"Do you want to go home?"

"Yes. Now."

"Hoke, but I must let Hattak Chula know."

Funi Man stood and made his way through the crowd. Hattak Chula was surrounded by councilmen and -women and their families. Everyone had a full dish in front of them. Funi Man nodded and waved away the many invitations to sit and join them. He knelt by Hattak Chula and whispered in his ear. "Just a moment, please. I need to speak to you."

Hattak Chula stood and wrapped his arm around Funi Man's shoulder. He gently pulled him away from the crowd. "What is wrong?"

"Nothing is wrong. Why are you asking me that?"

"Because I have been your friend for forty years, and I know you." Funi Man closed his eyes, and his head fell to his chest. "And I know you will tell me the truth and trust me to keep it," continued Hattak Chula.

"We need to go home," Funi Man said. "Shonti says someone is on her land."

"Shonti says there is danger?" Hattak Chula asked.

Funi Man tightened his lips and nodded. "Yes."

"You want me to make an excuse for you, so no one will notice your going?"

"Yes."

"Funi Man, I know that Shonti has her ways. We have ours as well, and I must protect this town."

"That is why I am coming to you," said Funi Man. "We have to hurry, please."

"Hoke. I will keep the celebration going. But you will be followed quietly by five of our best men."

"Yakoke."

"My friend," Hattak Chula said, gripping Funi Man's

shoulder with a strong hand, "you will be safe. The sun will rise on a good day for you and Shonti. Know this. I am so thankful for this time."

Funi Man nodded and turned to go. He found Shonti leaning against a tree and clutching her side. Her face was etched in pain.

"I spoke to Hattak Chula," Funi Man said. "He will tell the others you are tired and ready to be home, so no one will be alarmed."

"What else?" asked Shonti.

"He will send men to follow us. You will never see them."

"I hope they're not afraid of snakes," said Shonti.

Funi Man's jaw dropped. He had not thought of this! "I must really be getting old," he muttered under his breath. At that moment six large rattlesnakes slithered across the grounds, relieved and grateful to return to their true state—the hissing, crawling, and venomously poisonous friends and protectors of Ohoyo Hoshonti, Cloud Woman, better known as Shonti.

Funi Man and Shonti helped each other weave through the crowd, smiling and waving and avoiding their closest friends so no one would worry. When they arrived at the edge of the field, Funi Man helped Shonti mount his pony. He flung his throbbing leg over Hawkeye's back and eased onto the saddle.

"Hoke, Hawkeye, let's get moving," he said, patting his neck.

Soon they were topping the hill overlooking Shonti's land. At first Funi Man saw nothing unusual, but Shonti lunged forward in the saddle.

"Owww!" she cried.

"Chim achukma?" Funi Man asked. "Are you hoke?"

"Ahm achukma hoke," Shonti said, nodding quickly and pointing to the adjoining hill. "There they are."

"By the spring," Funi Man said. He squinted and covered his eyes to block the bright moonlight. "No. Not him."

"Who is it?" asked Shonti.

"The field guard from the plantation. You know him. Bledsoe."

"Bledsoe is on my land?"

"Yes. And that boy Harold is with him. Here, take my hand." Funi Man helped Shonti down from Hawkeye and led her to a sitting place. "Stay here, please. Let me do this, will you?"

"Yes, Funi Man, but be very careful."

"I will only listen," he said. "For now, only listening."

Funi Man ignored the pain in his knee. He sprinted, circling the hilltop. He arrived as Harold and Bledsoe were dipping water from the spring with cupped hands. He crept close enough to make out their words.

"You say that is the largest loblolly pine in Choctaw country?" asked Harold, pointing to a giant specimen of a tree on the opposite shore.

"Yes, and I doubt you'll see one this big anywhere," Bledsoe replied. He drank from the spring and wiped his mouth with his sleeve.

Why are they here? Funi Man asked himself. The answer soon came.

"When I let Mr. Kendall know about this land," Bledsoe said, "he will make it ours."

"And how can he do that?" asked Harold.

"With treaties," said Bledsoe. "You can always find someone to sign the treaty. Especially if they are surrounded by guns."

CHAPTER 50

Moonlight Chase

Martha Tom, Lil Mo, and their families sat down at a table covered with food. "Koi Losa, Joseph, come join us!" Lil Mo shouted.

"Look at all that food," said Joseph, with big eyes and a wide-open mouth.

"Try the pudding," said Lil Mo. "It's my favorite."

"Not as good as the banaha bread," said Koi Losa.

"And your mother made her first pot of pashofa corn soup," said Lil Mo's father.

The families surrounded a large table, and everyone talked at the same time. They laughed and waved their arms, feasting on deer meat, banaha bread, pashofa corn soup, blackberry pudding, wild onions, beans, and much more.

When all tummies were full, Martha Tom crept

behind Lil Mo. "You still can't catch me," she whispered. She pinched him on the shoulder, waved her dress in his face, and darted to the woods.

"I can catch you with my eyes closed!" said Lil Mo, leaping up from his chair.

Martha Tom ducked behind a thick red oak and slapped her hand to her mouth to stop a giggle. She watched as Lil Mo ran by, looking left and right but missing her completely. She counted slowly to ten: "Achvffa, tuklo, tuchina, ushta, tahlapi, hannali, ontuklo, ontuchina, chakkali, pokkoli."

When she was certain Lil Mo was out of sight, she jumped to her feet and shouted, "Lil Mo! I'm over here!"

Without waiting to see if he'd heard her, she dashed to the trees, the thick and shadowy pines. For half an hour Martha Tom led Lil Mo on a frightening chase in the dark, as deeper into the woods she ran. But the darkness was not her destination. She loved the water, the glow and ripple of the river.

"To Shonti's spring," she whispered to herself. "I'll take Lil Mo to Shonti's spring! We can watch the moonlight on the water." She turned to the west.

"You'll never catch me now," she called over her shoulder, laughing and leaping and dancing through the trees. "I thought you were faster than that!"

Lil Mo *was* faster. He watched her top the hill and dash

to Shonti's spring, her dress flying and her arms stretched out like a bird in flight.

I'll beat her there! he thought.

Lil Mo sped down the hill, lured by the golden waters, lost in the moonlit night of his dreams. He stopped only when he reached the muddy shore. He leaned against a tall, thin pine, huffing and puffing and smiling at the thought of surprising Martha Tom.

He felt no fear when a hand reached from behind the tree and grabbed his collar.

"You can't outrun me!" he said, expecting laughter and his first-ever true hug from Martha Tom.

But the hand that gripped his shoulder was not Martha Tom's. The fingers were strong, and the voice was deep. "Look what we found. You're a long way from home, aren't you, little slave boy?" Bledsoe stepped out from the shadows. Lil Mo struggled, but another man held him by the waist against the tree.

"I have a pistol at your head, so running is not a good idea," said Bledsoe. Lil Mo felt the end of the pistol barrel, hard against his cheekbone. He flinched, and Bledsoe grabbed his throat, pinning him against the tree.

———

Martha Tom slowed to a walk. She had never been this

alone with Lil Mo. *No more teasing and pretending we don't like each other*, she thought. *I will someday marry Lil Mo.* She found a large, flat rock near the water and sat down to wait.

"Oh," said Bledsoe, spotting Martha Tom in the distance. "So you are not alone, Lil Mo. What do you think, Harold? Should she find his body, or maybe watch him die?"

"She is the girl who led his family across the river," said Harold. "I'll get her."

"Leave her alone!" said Lil Mo.

The sky darkened with shapes and shadows of owls against the moonlight, owls answering the death call. Martha Tom stopped when she heard the owl. She slowly backed away, but when she turned to run, Harold blocked her path.

"You looking for Lil Mo?" he asked. "I can help you." Harold gripped her wrist, hard, and dragged Martha Tom up the hill. He flung her against the tree trunk to stand with Lil Mo.

"Lil Mo, the others are coming," Martha Tom said. "Koi Losa is close by. You know he would never let you wander off alone, never."

"I welcome this Choctaw boy, this friend of Lil Mo's," said Bledsoe. "He needs a lesson in what happens when you help runaway slaves."

Bledsoe laid his pistol on the ground. From a pouch behind his back he unsheathed a hunting knife. He placed the blade against Lil Mo's throat.

"Does the sight of blood make you squirm, Martha Tom? You people butcher deer. You must see blood. You are about to know what human blood looks like. It has its very own smell, too. One you will never forget."

He slid the blade lightly across Lil Mo's neck, drawing a spot of blood.

"No!" Martha Tom shouted. "He has done nothing to you!"

"He has done more to me than you will ever know," said Bledsoe.

"These woods and fields are full of Choctaws, looking for us," she said. "You will never get away."

As darkness settled in the pine trees, and evil men stood in the shadows, a soft light crept across the waters. Lil Mo saw it first, the green glow of the lanterns. The soft green light of the Bohpoli rose from the depths of the spring.

A new voice joined the circle. "If you want to see the morning, you will drop your knife." Hattak Chula and five young Choctaws, armed with shotguns, stepped from the woods.

"You can do nothing to me," Bledsoe said. "You know who I am."

"Yes," said Hattak Chula. "You are a trespasser on Choctaw land. You are threatening to kill a citizen of our nation. You will drop your weapon. Now."

Bledsoe looked about him. Funi Man appeared next, and behind him came Joseph.

"You will pay," said Bledsoe, seeing Joseph.

"You are in Choctaw Nation now," said Funi Man. "Your power lies across the river. You had no right to cross it."

Unseen by the gathering, Treda and Lavester slipped into the woods and neared the tree. "They will not have my son," Treda whispered.

"No. Not tonight, not ever," Lavester said. "Bledsoe will never harm a member of our family, never again."

Treda spotted Bledsoe's pistol on the ground. She lowered herself till she lay flat against the forest floor. As quietly and quickly as she dared, she crawled to the base of the tree and took the pistol. She leaned her back against the trunk and pushed herself to standing.

"You had no right to help slaves cross the river," said Bledsoe to the Choctaws. "This boy belongs to the plantation, and I will take his body with me when I return."

Treda stepped out from behind the tree and spoke in a voice loud enough for all to hear. "You will not harm my son," she said, holding the pistol to Bledsoe's head.

Bledsoe flinched, but only for a moment.

"Maybe I will not harm him," he said, "now that you are here. I have a better idea. You make the choice. You are free, are you not? Free to choose? Your son may live, and you, and Joseph. No one will die tonight. You simply must return to the fields, to your old job. Or would you rather stay here and grieve over the body of your son, the son you let die?"

"No!" The booming voice of Lavester rang out. "We will never go back. Do you hear me? Never! You have no power here."

"Then watch your son die," said Bledsoe. He grabbed Lil Mo by the hair, digging in his fingers, and pulled Lil Mo's head back.

Treda's hand shook. She took a deep breath, steadied herself, and prepared to fire.

"You know better than to kill me," Bledsoe hissed. "You want blood? You kill me, and these fields will flow with Choctaw blood. You kill me, and you start a war."

Lil Mo looked to Funi Man. No one else heard the low growling from the foot of the tree. Together Lil Mo and Funi Man mouthed the words they were thinking, over and over.

If you love your dog, truly love and care for him, when your life is in danger, your dog will be there for you.

The green light grew to a power Lil Mo had never imagined. The sky shone green, the waters, the air, till every face and tree and stone pulsed with the Bohpoli light. Bledsoe froze, and Ofijo leapt.

No blood touched the earth on this green Miracle Night. Ofijo leapt not for the wrist of Bledsoe, holding the knife to Lil Mo's throat. He leapt for the hand of Treda. Her pistol exploded and sent a harmless bullet deep into the trunk of the red oak tree. Hearing the pistol blast, Bledsoe turned to the sound, where Lavester waited.

He cocked his fist and knocked Bledsoe to the ground. "I have wanted to do this for years," Lavester said.

Lil Mo ran into the outstretched arms of Funi Man, his Choctaw uncle.

With Bledsoe fallen, Harold ran to the woods, where Koi Losa waited. He leapt from a low-hanging tree limb and tackled Harold. They rolled to the ground, and Harold covered his face, shouting and afraid.

"I don't have a gun! Please don't hurt me."

"Brave Harold," said Koi Losa, "I would never hurt you." He pulled Harold's pistol from his belt. "And I know you don't have your gun. I already found it."

CHAPTER 51

Crossing a River Is a Beautiful Thing

By midmorning Hattak Chula, accompanied by twenty armed Choctaws, crossed over the Bok Chitto River bridge, ten miles upstream. Long before they reached the plantation, Mr. Kendall knew of their coming. He sent four house servants to greet the Choctaw party.

"We are here to discuss the recent events between employees of the plantation and the Choctaw Nation," Hattak Chula announced. "Please inform the owners."

Well-dressed household workers tied the Choctaw ponies to a railing. Mr. Kendall soon appeared at the door.

"You may enter," he said to Hattak Chula.

"Some members of our council will also be present," said Hattak Chula, "and the others will stand guard outside."

"There is no need for guards," said Mr. Kendall. "You are welcome here." Hattak Chula did not reply. He simply nodded to Blue Doe, Funi Man, and two other councilmen.

As the Choctaws stepped inside the plantation house, they tried to hide their wonder at the richly furnished greeting room. Shiny silk curtains and large painted portraits hung from the walls. A marble sculpture of a horse and chariot stood in a corner.

Mr. Kendall led the Choctaws to a large table in a side room. When all were seated, he spoke first. "You have one of my employees, Mr. Bledsoe."

"We do, and are prepared to return him to your care," said Hattak Chula. "Regarding the family who crossed the river, they will not be returned."

Mr. Kendall bristled. "They are my property," he said in a quiet and threatening voice.

"They are Choctaw citizens now," said Hattak Chula. "We will protect them."

Mr. Kendall pushed back his chair and clenched the table, but Hattak Chula lifted his hand, saying, "Hear me out, please. Still your anger and hear me out. We are prepared to offer you a large piece of Choctaw river bottom land in return for the family. It should cover whatever costs you bear in the loss of the workers."

Mr. Kendall looked about the room. He walked to

312

the window, opened the curtains, and watched the field workers for a long while before speaking.

"We will abide by our agreement," he said. "But this will be the end of it. I will respect your laws, and you must respect ours."

Hattak Chula rose. "We will abide by our agreement. Your men will remain on this side of the river, and we will be at peace."

Mr. Kendall nodded, and the two leaders shook hands, sealing their promise.

"I have one more request, if you would hear me out," said Hattak Chula.

"Yes? What more would you like?"

"You have one among you, a household worker, who does not by law belong to you."

"Oh?" said Mr. Kendall, raising his eyebrows.

"Yes. In good faith, I have brought a wagonload of tools, saws and hatchets, useful tools for the plantation; tools for clearing your new land. You may keep the two ponies pulling the wagon, and the wagon as well."

"What would you like in return?" asked Mr. Kendall.

"My daughter," said Hattak Chula. "She was taken from us years ago. I would like her back."

A crash came from the adjoining room.

"Watch yourself!" shouted Miss Bonnie, Mr. Kendall's elderly mother.

Tisha stepped into the room and greeted her father. She made no effort to hide the tears flowing down her cheeks.

"You come back here!" Miss Bonnie said.

Mr. Kendall shook his head. "We will find someone else to do my mother's bidding. Go pack your clothes and begone," he said to Tisha.

"I can go now," she replied. "I have no need of my plantation clothes. I will be taken care of in Choctaw town."

"Yes, you will be taken care of," said Hattak Chula. "Choctaws take care of their own. We are all in this together. Ilvppa ittibai foyuka."

As per the agreement, Hattak Chula delivered Bledsoe to Mr. Kendall that very afternoon. Bledsoe would spend five days in the barn jail before being relieved of his duties at the plantation. Word among the Choctaws was that he made his way to New Orleans.

Though plantation owners still eyed Choctaw land, Lil Mo and his family felt safe in Choctaw town. For the first time in their lives, Lavester and Treda had a home of their own. Their son, Lil Mo, was promised in marriage to Martha Tom, and Angel had found many friends.

Lil Mo never crossed the Bok Chitto River again, though Joseph often did. One evening, over steaming hot cups of pashofa, Lil Mo, Joseph, Koi Losa, and Funi Man sat together with the newest Choctaw hero—Ofijo.

"Funi Man?" said Lil Mo, rubbing Ofijo's ears.

"Yes, Lil Mo."

"Why did Ofijo jump at my mother? Why didn't he bite Bledsoe?"

"If Ofijo had gone for Bledsoe, what would your mother have done?"

"I guess she would have shot Bledsoe," said Lil Mo. "We would not have to worry about him again, not ever."

"You say that now, Lil Mo. But if your mother killed Bledsoe, she would worry about that day for the rest of her life. He might be a bad man, an evil man, but your mother would forever grieve the day she killed him."

"Funi Man, you are right again," said Lil Mo. "How did you get to be so smart?"

"He didn't use to be smart," said Koi Losa.

"What happened?" asked Joseph.

"He finally started listening to me," Koi Losa said.

"Or maybe he started listening to *me*!" said a voice from the shadows. Everyone jumped, then turned to see Martha Tom. "I like pashofa, too," she said, holding out an empty cup.

When the laughter settled, Funi Man spoke. "You young folks have grown so much. I am very proud of you all. Wanna know something else, Lil Mo?"

"Yes, Funi Man."

"I might be old, very old, but I am determined to live long enough to see your wedding day."

"You will," said Lil Mo.

"Yes," said Funi Man, "because if your wedding day is anything like mine, I don't want to miss it."

"Now that's funny!" said Lil Mo.

"And very, very Choctaw," Funi Man replied.

Glossary and Pronunciation Guide

achvffa, tuklo, tuchina, ushta, tahlapi, hannali, ontuklo, ontuchina, chakkali, pokkoli (ah-CHUF-fah, TOOK-a-low, toe-CHE-nah, OOSH-tah, tah-THA-peh, HAHN-NAH-leh, own-TOOK-low, chahk-KAH-lih, pohk-KO-lih): one, two, three, four, five, six, seven, eight, nine, ten

achukma (ah-CHOOK-mah): good

Ahm achukma hoke (ahm ah-CHOOK-mah hoh-KAY): I'm doing good.

alikchi (ah-LICK-chih): medicine person, traditional doctor

amafo (ah-MAH-foh): my grandfather; grandfather

Balili! (bah-LIH-lih): Run!

banaha (bah-NAH-hah): shuck bread

Bohpoli (BOH-poe-lih): little people with magical powers, like the Irish Leprechauns

Chim achukma? (cheem ah-CHOOK-mah): Are you good?

Chi pisa la chike (chee PEH-sah LAH chee-KAY): Until we meet again.

funi (FUH-nee): squirrel

halito (hah-lih-TOE): hello

hoke (hoh-KAY): good (okay in today's English)

Holitopa (hoh-lih-TOE-pah): sacred, holy, esteemed

Ilvppa ittibai foyuka (eel-LAHP-pah it-tee-BYE foh-YOH-ka): We are all in this together.

iskuli (es-KUL-lih): money

Koi Losa (ko-we LOW-sah): dark or black panther

ma (MAH): exclamation ("Oh!"); Shilombish Holitopa Ma means "Oh Holy Spirit."

nahullo/nahollo★ (nah-HO-lo): white person

ofi (OH-feh): dog

Ofi okpulo (OH-feh oak-PUH-low): bad, rascally dog

okla chukma (OAK-lah CHOOK-mah): good people

onnahinli chukma (own-nah-HEN-lih CHOOK-ma): good morning

Owa Naholo (OH-wah nah-HO-lo): fish people

pashofa (pah-SHOH-fah): corn soup; older Choctaw Elders uses **tanchi la bona** (TANN-chee lah BOHN-nah)

shilombish (she-LOHM-bish): spirit

tobi walhali (TOE-bih wah-THA-lih): boiled beans

yakoke (yah-koh-KAY): thank you

yannash (yahn-NASH): buffalo

★Publisher's note: Research reveals that the correct spelling is "nahollo," but the information came to the author's attention too late to fix it in the main body of the text. We note it here for accuracy and will correct it in future printings.

Song translation from pages 44 and 45:

Nitak ishtayo pickmano,
Chisus–ut minitit,
Umala Holitopama,
Chohot ayalaski.

When the last day comes, Jesus is coming.
I shall go with him to that holy place,
to where I will arrive.

Author's Note

Dear Reader,

As a member of the Choctaw Nation and the fortunate nephew of uncles who loved to share stories, I learned long ago that the truth about most Native American history is not to be found in books. From researching the Trail of Tears, I learned that Indians in the Southeastern United States have been fearful to share their past. And why? For one hundred years, from the Trail to a document signed by President Franklin Delano Roosevelt, it was basically illegal to be of Native heritage in the South. If you were of Indian blood, you could have everything you owned, your home, livestock, all belongings, taken from you, and you would be sent penniless to Indian Territory, Oklahoma.

In 1993, I began my research with Mississippi Choctaws—those who had survived the dangers of a century. I spent several weeks a year, sometimes months, getting to know other Choctaws and their families and tape-recording their stories—stories that later became the basis for my master's degree thesis at the University of Oklahoma. A tribal elder named Archie Mingo became a dear friend, and soon we both recognized an almost divine foundation to our meetings. From the first day I met him, every time I stepped foot on the soil of Mississippi—whether driving along the coast to Alabama, or filling my rented car with gasoline just south of Memphis, Tennessee—I would "bump into" Archie, totally unplanned and unexpected. Oftentimes our meetings would occur several hours from his home in Philadelphia, Mississippi.

It was Archie who told me of the river Bok Chitto and the enslaved people who lived "on the other side." He also spoke of Choctaws who dug basements under their homes to hide escaping slaves. Though I later learned of wealthy Choctaws who lived to the north and owned slaves, Archie never mentioned them to me, but rather told of family and friends of generations long ago, who risked their lives to free slaves. This novel and my picture book, *Crossing Bok Chitto*, draw upon his stories.

Archie's stories were documented in the Indian way, told and retold and then passed on by uncles and grand-mothers. Native Americans live in a world that often accepts the spoken word as the final authority. Even today, many Choctaws are likely to trust a story told to them by another Choctaw more than anything they read on the printed page. This book extends my tribute in *Crossing Bok Chitto* to the Choctaws, Cherokees, Creeks,

Chickasaws, and Seminoles—and Indians of every nation—who aided people escaping from bondage.

We Natives must continue recounting our past and, hopefully from this book, non-Indians might realize the sweet and secret fire that drives the Indian heart. We are proud of who we are. We are determined that our way, shared by many of all races—a way of respect for others and the land we live on—will prevail.

Tim Tingle
December 2018

Acknowledgments

Stone River Crossing began in the latter years of the last century, as I stood with Choctaw elder Archie Mingo atop Nainah Waiyah, our sacred mound in Central Mississippi. He pointed across the road to a river flowing through a wooded area, and told me of Choctaws helping slaves escape. I soon began performing "Crossing Bok Chitto," a fictional story based on this experience, at storytelling festivals across the United States. I am forever indebted to fellow storytellers and friends Doc Moore, Elizabeth Ellis, Bobby Norfolk, Donna Ingham, Consuelo Samarippa, and so many others, especially Joe Bruchac, who encouraged me to write the story.

Crossing Bok Chitto became my first picture book, won numerous national awards, and eventually inspired *Stone River Crossing*. I am forever grateful to Cinco Puntos Press and Bobby and Lee Byrd for their faith in my work. Dr. Geary Hobson of the University of Oklahoma was my strongest inspiration to write, and Greg Rodgers, my Choctaw writing partner, was tough and tender and just what a writer needs for more than a decade. I also want to thank Debbie Reese, a friend and colleague in the drive to educate, and my fellow-Texan and Chero-kee writer friend, Cynthia Leitich Smith. Many thanks to writer Dawn Quigley, my inspiring Turtle Mountain Band of Ojibwe friend, for providing the best ride-from-the-airport in years. To Susan Feller, Walter Echo-Hawk, Mary Ellen Meredith, Melissa Brodt, and all of my friends from ATALM, I hold you close. My son, Dr. Jacob Tingle, and "duh boyz," grandsons Finnegan and Niko, are my primary target audience in everything I write. And if you ever see me alone, ask me about my creative writing instructor, Dr. Robert Fergusen of the University of Oklahoma, and how his ghost launched my career. Bill McKee, Stacy Wells, Lisa Eister, and fellow Trojans Bob Willard, Joy Beck, Irma Schelsteder, Jackie Spangler, Patty Shiver, Marsha Rudolf, Chris and Bobby Spiers, Pam Vanway, Paulette George, you keep me going.

To Chief Greg Pyle of the Choctaw Nation of Oklahoma, who asked me to tell "Crossing Bok Chitto" before his 2005 State of the Nation address following Hurricane Katrina, in which he announced lodging and meals would be provided for all people fleeing the devastation. Yakoke to Chief Gary Batton, Lisa Reed, Judy Allen, and the thousands of Choctaws who have supported my work, and especially Leroy Sealy, my Choctaw language teacher.

Immense gratitude to Stacy Whitman, my editor, and my agent Andrea Cascardi, for your patience with a stubborn old Choctaw.